Nemesis

To Shirley
with love on
your 80tt

Heb
x

BOOKS BY PHILIP ROTH

ZUCKERMAN BOOKS
The Ghost Writer
Zuckerman Unbound
The Anatomy Lesson
The Prague Orgy

The Counterlife

American Pastoral
I Married a Communist
The Human Stain

Exit Ghost

ROTH BOOKS
The Facts · Deception
Patrimony · Operation Shylock
The Plot Against America

KEPESH BOOKS
The Breast
The Professor of Desire
The Dying Animal

NEMESES: SHORT NOVELS
Everyman · Indignation
The Humbling · Nemesis

MISCELLANY
Reading Myself and Others
Shop Talk

OTHER BOOKS
Goodbye, Columbus · Letting Go
When She Was Good · Portnoy's Complaint · Our Gang
The Great American Novel · My Life as a Man
Sabbath's Theater

Nemesis

Philip Roth

JONATHAN CAPE
LONDON

Published by Jonathan Cape 2010

2 4 6 8 10 9 7 5 3

First published in Great Britain in 2010 by
Jonathan Cape
Random House, 20 Vauxhall Bridge Road,
London SW1V 2SA

www.rbooks.co.uk

Addresses for companies within The Random House Group Limited can be
found at: www.randomhouse.co.uk/offices.htm

The Random House Group Limited Reg. No. 954009

A CIP catalogue record for this book
is available from the British Library

ISBN 9780224089531

The Random House Group Limited makes every effort to ensure that the
papers used in its books are made from trees that have been legally
sourced from well-managed and credibly certified forests.
Our paper procurement policy can be found at:
www.randomhouse.co.uk/paper.htm

Printed and bound in Great Britain by
Clays Ltd, St Ives PLC

For H. L:

ACKNOWLEDGMENTS

Sources from which I've drawn information include *The Throws Manual*, by George D. Dunn, Jr., and Kevin McGill; *The Encyclopedia of Religion*, edited by Mircea Eliade; *Teaching Springboard Diving*, by Anne Ross Fairbanks; *Camp Management* and *Recreational Programs for Summer Camps*, by H. W. Gibson; *Dirt and Disease*, by Naomi Rogers; *Polio's Legacy*, by Edmund J. Sass; *A Paralyzing Fear*, by Nina Gilden Seavey, Jane S. Smith, and Paul Wagner; *Polio Voices*, by Julie Silver and Daniel Wilson; and *A Manufactured Wilderness*, by Abigail Van Slyck. Particularly useful was *The Book of Woodcraft*, by Ernest Thompson Seton, from which I have liberally drawn on pages 209–214, and *Manual of the Woodcraft Indians*, also by Seton, from which I have quoted on pages 146–147.

Nemesis

1

Equatorial Newark

THE FIRST CASE of polio that summer came early in June, right after Memorial Day, in a poor Italian neighborhood crosstown from where we lived. Over in the city's southwestern corner, in the Jewish Weequahic section, we heard nothing about it, nor did we hear anything about the next dozen cases scattered singly throughout Newark in nearly every neighborhood but ours. Only by the Fourth of July, when there were already forty cases reported in the city, did an article appear on the front page of the evening paper, titled "Health Chief Puts Parents on Polio Alert," in which Dr. William Kittell, superintendent of the Board of Health, was quoted as cautioning parents to monitor their children closely and to contact a physician if a child exhibited symptoms such as headache,

sore throat, nausea, stiff neck, joint pain, or fever.
Though Dr. Kittell acknowledged that forty polio
cases was more than twice as many as normally reported this early in the polio season, he wanted it
clearly understood that the city of 429,000 was by
no means suffering from what could be character-
ized as an epidemic of poliomyelitis. This summer
as every summer, there was reason for concern and
for the proper hygienic precautions to be taken, but
there was as yet no cause for the sort of alarm that
had been displayed by parents, "justifiably enough,"
twenty-eight years earlier, during the largest outbreak of the disease ever reported—the 1916 polio
epidemic in the northeastern United States, when
there had been more than 27,000 cases, with 6,000
deaths. In Newark there had been 1,360 cases and
363 deaths.

Now even in a year with an average number of
cases, when the chances of contracting polio were
much reduced from what they'd been back in 1916,
a paralytic disease that left a youngster permanently
disabled and deformed or unable to breathe outside
a cylindrical metal respirator tank known as an iron
lung—or that could lead from paralysis of the respiratory muscles to death—caused the parents in

our neighborhood considerable apprehension and marred the peace of mind of children who were free of school for the summer months and able to play outdoors all day and into the long twilit evenings. Concern for the dire consequences of falling seriously ill from polio was compounded by the fact that no medicine existed to treat the disease and no vaccine to produce immunity. Polio—or infantile paralysis, as it was called when the disease was thought to infect mainly toddlers—could befall anyone, for no apparent reason. Though children up to sixteen were usually the sufferers, adults too could become severely infected, as had the current president of the United States.

Franklin Delano Roosevelt, polio's most renowned victim, had contracted the disease as a vigorous man of thirty-nine and subsequently had to be supported when he walked and, even then, had to wear heavy steel-and-leather braces from his hips to his feet to enable him to stand. The charitable institution that FDR founded while he was in the White House, the March of Dimes, raised money for research and for financial assistance to the families of the stricken; though partial or even full recovery was possible, it was often only after months or years of expensive hospital therapy and rehabilitation. During the annual fund drive, America's young donated their dimes at school to help in the fight against the disease, they dropped their dimes into collection cans passed around by ushers in movie theaters, and posters announcing "You Can Help, Too!" and "Help Fight Polio!" appeared on the walls of stores and offices and in the corridors of schools across the country, posters of children in wheelchairs—a pretty little girl wearing leg braces shyly sucking her thumb, a clean-cut little boy with leg braces heroically smiling with hope— posters that made the possibility of getting the disease seem all the more frighteningly real to otherwise healthy children.

Summers were steamy in low-lying Newark, and because the city was partially ringed by extensive wetlands—a major source of malaria back when that, too, was an unstoppable disease—there were swarms of mosquitoes to be swatted and slapped away whenever we sat on beach chairs in the alleys and driveways at night, seeking refuge out of doors from our sweltering flats, where there was nothing but a cold shower and ice water to mitigate the hellish heat. This was before the advent of home air conditioning, when a small black electric fan, set on a table to stir up a breeze indoors, offered little relief once the temperature reached the high nineties, as it did repeatedly that summer for stretches of a week or ten days. Outdoors, people lit citronella candles and sprayed with cans of the insecticide Flit to keep at bay the mosquitoes and flies that were known to have carried malaria, yellow fever, and typhoid fever and were believed by many, beginning with Newark's Mayor Drummond, who launched a citywide "Swat the Fly" campaign, to carry polio. When a fly or a mosquito managed to penetrate the screens of a family's flat or fly in through an open door, the insect would be doggedly hunted down with fly swatter and Flit out of fear that by alighting with its germ-laden legs on one of the household's sleeping children it would infect the youngster with polio. Since nobody then knew the source of the contagion, it was possible to grow suspicious of almost anything, including the bony alley cats that invaded our backyard garbage cans and the haggard stray dogs that slinked hungrily around the houses and defecated all over the sidewalk and street and the pigeons that cooed in the gables of the houses and dirtied front stoops with their chalky droppings. In the first month of the outbreak—before it was acknowledged as an epidemic by the Board of Health—the sanitation department set about systematically to exterminate the city's huge population of alley cats, even though no one knew whether they had any more to do with polio than domesticated house cats.

What people did know was that the disease was highly contagious and might be passed to the healthy by mere physical proximity to those already infected. For this reason, as the number of cases steadily mounted in the city—and communal fear with it—many children in our neighborhood found themselves prohibited by their parents from using the big public pool at Olympic Park in nearby Irvington, forbidden to go to the local "air-cooled" movie theaters, and forbidden to take the bus downtown or to travel Down Neck to Wilson Avenue to see our minor league team, the Newark Bears, play baseball at Ruppert Stadium. We were warned not to use public toilets or public drinking fountains or to swig a drink out of someone else's soda-pop bottle or to get a chill or to play with strangers or to borrow books from the public library or to talk on a public pay phone or to buy food from a street vendor or to eat until we had cleaned our hands thoroughly with soap and water. We were to wash all fruit and vegetables before we ate them, and we were to keep our distance from anyone who looked sick or complained of any of polio's telltale symptoms.

Escaping the city's heat entirely and being sent off to a summer camp in the mountains or the countryside was considered a child's best protection against catching polio. So too was spending the summer some sixty miles away at the Jersey Shore. A family who could afford it rented a bedroom with kitchen privileges in a rooming house in Bradley Beach, a strip of sand, boardwalk, and cottages a mile long that had already been popular for several decades among North Jersey Jews. There the mother and the children would go to the beach to breathe in the fresh, fortifying ocean air all week long and be joined on weekends and vacations by the father. Of course, cases of polio were known to crop up in summer camps as they did in the shore's seaside towns, but because they were nothing like as numerous as those reported back in Newark, it was widely believed that, whereas city surroundings, with their unclean pavements and stagnant air, facilitated contagion, settling within sight or sound of the sea or off in the country or up in the mountains afforded as good a guarantee as there was of evading the disease.

So the privileged lucky ones disappeared from the city for the summer while the rest of us remained behind to do exactly what we shouldn't, given that "overexertion" was suspected of being yet another possible cause of polio: we played inning after inning and game after game of softball on the baking asphalt of the school playground, running around all day in the extreme heat, drinking thirstily from the forbidden water fountain, between innings seated on a bench crushed up against one another, clutching in our laps the well-worn, grimy mitts we used out in the field to mop the sweat off our foreheads and to keep it from running into our eyes— clowning and carrying on in our soaking polo shirts and our smelly sneakers, unmindful of how our imprudence might be dooming any one of us to lifelong incarceration in an iron lung and the realization of the body's most dreadful fears.

Only a dozen or so girls ever appeared at the playground, mainly kids of eight or nine who could usually be seen jumping rope where far center field dropped off into a narrow school street closed to traffic. When the girls weren't jumping rope they used the street for hopscotch and running-bases and playing jacks or for happily bouncing a pink rubber ball at their feet all day long. Sometimes when the girls jumping rope played double dutch, twirling two ropes in opposite directions, one of the boys would rush up unbidden and, elbowing aside the girl who was about to jump, leap in and mockingly start bellowing the girls' favorite jumping song while deliberately entangling himself in their flying ropes. "H, my name is Hippopotamus—!" The girls would holler at him "Stop it! Stop it!" and call out for help from the playground director, who had only to shout from wherever he was on the playground to the troublemaker (most days it was the same boy), "Cut it out, Myron! Leave the girls alone or you're going home!" With that, the uproar subsided. Soon the jump ropes were once again snappily turning in the air and the chanting taken up anew by one jumper after another:

A, my name is Agnes
And my husband's name is Alphonse,
We come from Alabama
And we bring back apples!

B, my name is Bev
And my husband's name is Bill,
We come from Bermuda
And we bring back beets!
C, my name is . . .

With their childish voices, the girls encamped at the far edge of the playground improvised their way from A to Z and back again, alliterating the nouns at the end of the line, sometimes preposterously, each time around. Leaping and darting about with excitement—except when Myron Kopferman and his like would apishly interfere—they exhibited astounding energy; unless they were summoned by the playground director to retreat to the shade of the school because of the heat, they didn't vacate that street from the Friday in June when the spring term ended to the Tuesday after Labor Day when the fall term began and they could jump rope only after school and at recess.

The playground director that year was Bucky Cantor, who, because of poor vision that necessitated his wearing thick eyeglasses, was one of the few young men around who wasn't off fighting in the war. During the previous school year, Mr. Cantor had become the new phys ed teacher at Chan-

cellor Avenue School and so already knew many of
us who habituated the playground from the gym
classes he taught. He was twenty-three that summer, a graduate of South Side, Newark's mixed-race,
mixed-religion high school, and Panzer College of
Physical Education and Hygiene in East Orange.
He stood slightly under five feet five inches tall,
and though he was a superior athlete and strong
competitor, his height, combined with his poor vision, had prevented him from playing college-level
football, baseball, or basketball and restricted his
intercollegiate sports activity to throwing the javelin and lifting weights. Atop his compact body was
a good-sized head formed of emphatically slanting and sloping components: wide pronounced
cheekbones, a steep forehead, an angular jaw, and
a long straight nose with a prominent bridge that
lent his profile the sharpness of a silhouette en-
graved on a coin. His full lips were as well defined
as his muscles, and his complexion was tawny year-
round. Since adolescence he had worn his hair in
a military-style crewcut. You particularly noticed
his ears with that haircut, not because they were
unduly large, which they were not, not necessarily because they were joined so closely to his head,

but because, seen from the side, they were shaped much like the ace of spades in a pack of cards, or the wings on the winged feet of mythology, with topmost tips that weren't rounded off, as most ears are, but came nearly to a point. Before his grandfather dubbed him Bucky, he was known briefly as Ace to his childhood street pals, a nickname inspired not merely by his precocious excellence at sports but by the uncommon configuration of those ears.

Altogether the oblique planes of his face gave the smoky gray eyes back of his glasses—eyes long and narrow like an Asian's—a deeply pocketed look, as though they were not so much set as cratered in the skull. The voice emerging from this precisely delineated face was, unexpectedly, rather high-pitched, but that did not diminish the force of his appearance. His was the cast-iron, wear-resistant, strikingly bold face of a sturdy young man you could rely on.

ONE AFTERNOON early in July, two cars full of Italians from East Side High, boys anywhere from fifteen to eighteen, drove in and parked at the top of the residential street back of the school, where the playground was situated. East Side was in the

Ironbound section, the industrial slum that had reported the most cases of polio in the city so far. As
soon as Mr. Cantor saw them pull up, he dropped
his mitt on the field—he was playing third base
in one of our pickup games—and trotted over to
where the ten strangers had emptied out of the two
cars. His athletic, pigeon-toed trot was already being imitated by the playground kids, as was his pur-
poseful way of lightly lifting himself as he moved
on the balls of his feet, and the slight sway, when
he walked, of his substantial shoulders. For some of
the boys his entire bearing had become theirs both
on and off the playing field.

"What do you fellows want here?" Mr. Cantor
said.

"We're spreadin' polio," one of the Italians replied. He was the one who'd come swaggering out
of the cars first. "Ain't that right?" he said, turning
to preen for the cohorts backing him up, who appeared right off to Mr. Cantor to be only too eager
to begin a brawl.

"You look more like you're spreadin' trouble,"
Mr. Cantor told him. "Why don't you head out of
here?"

"No, no," the Italian guy insisted, "not till we

spread some polio. We got it and you don't, so we thought we'd drive up and spread a little around." All the while he talked, he rocked back and forth on his heels to indicate how tough he was. The brazen ease of his thumbs tucked into the front two loops of his trousers served no less than his gaze to register his contempt.

"I'm playground director here," Mr. Cantor said, pointing back over his shoulder toward us kids. "I'm asking you to leave the vicinity of the playground. You've got no business here and I'm asking you politely to go. What do you say?"

"Since when is there a law against spreadin' polio, Mr. Playground Director?"

"Look, polio is not a joke. And there's a law against being a public nuisance. I don't want to have to call the police. How about leaving on your own, before I get the cops to escort you out of here?"

With this, the leader of the pack, who was easily half a foot taller than Mr. Cantor, took a step forward and spat on the pavement. He left a gob of viscous sputum splattered there, only inches from the tip of Mr. Cantor's sneakers.

"What's that mean?" Mr. Cantor asked him. His voice was still calm and, with his arms crossed tightly over his chest, he was the embodiment of immovability. No Ironbound roughnecks were going to get the better of him or come anywhere near his kids.

"I told you what it means. We're spreadin' polio. We don't want to leave you people out."

"Look, cut the 'you people' crap," Mr. Cantor said and took one quick, angry step forward, placing him only inches from the Italian's face. "I'll give you ten seconds to turn around and move everybody out of here."

The Italian smiled. He really hadn't stopped smiling since he'd gotten out of the car. "Then what?" he asked.

"I told you. I'm going to get the cops to get you out and keep you out."

Here the Italian guy spat again, this time just to the side of Mr. Cantor's sneakers, and Mr. Cantor called over to the boy who had been waiting to bat next in the game and who, like the rest of us, was silently watching Mr. Cantor face down the ten Italians. "Jerry," Mr. Cantor said, "run to my office. Telephone the police. Say you're calling for me. Tell them I need them."

"What are they going to do, lock me up?" the

chief Italian guy asked. "They gonna put me in the slammer for spitting on your precious Weequahic sidewalk? You own the sidewalk too, four eyes?"

Mr. Cantor didn't answer and just remained planted between the kids who'd been playing ball on the asphalt field behind him and the two carloads of Italian guys, still standing on the street at the edge of the playground as though each were about to drop the cigarette he was smoking and suddenly brandish a weapon. But by the time Jerry returned from Mr. Cantor's basement office—where, as instructed, he had telephoned the police—the two cars and their ominous occupants were gone. When the patrol car pulled up only minutes later, Mr. Cantor was able to give the cops the license plate numbers of both cars, which he'd memorized during the standoff. Only after the police had driven away did the kids back of the fence begin to ridicule the Italians.

It turned out that there was sputum spread over the wide area of pavement where the Italian guys had congregated, some twenty square feet of a wet, slimy, disgusting mess that certainly appeared to be an ideal breeding ground for disease. Mr. Cantor

had two of the boys go down in the school basement to find a couple of buckets and fill them with
hot water and ammonia in the janitor's room and
then slosh the water across the pavement until every inch of it was washed clean. The kids slosh-
ing away the slime reminded Mr. Cantor of how
he'd had to clean up after killing a rat at the back
of his grandfather's grocery store when he was ten
years old.

"Nothing to worry about," Mr. Cantor told the
boys. "They won't be back. That's just life," he said,
quoting a line favored by his grandfather, "there's
always something funny going on," and he rejoined
the game and play was resumed. The boys observing from the other side of the two-story-high
chainlink fence that enclosed the playground were
mightily impressed by Mr. Cantor's taking on the
Italians as he did. His confident, decisive manner,
his weightlifter's strength, his joining in every day
to enthusiastically play ball right alongside the rest
of us—all this had made him a favorite of the playground regulars from the day he'd arrived as director; but after the incident with the Italians he
became an outright hero, an idolized, protective,

heroic older brother, particularly to those whose own older brothers were off in the war.

It was later in the week that two of the boys who'd been at the playground when the Italians had come around didn't show up for a few days to play ball. On the first morning, both had awakened with high fevers and stiff necks, and by the second evening—having begun to grow helplessly weak in their arms and legs and to have difficulty breathing—had to be rushed to the hospital by ambulance. One of the boys, Herbie Steinmark, was a chubby, clumsy, amiable eighth grader who, because of his athletic ineptness, was usually assigned to play right field and bat last, and the other, Alan Michaels, also an eighth grader, was among the two or three best athletes on the playground and the boy who'd grown closest to Mr. Cantor. Herbie's and Alan's constituted the first cases of polio in the neighborhood. Within forty-eight hours there were eleven additional cases, and though none were kids who'd been at the playground that day, word spread through the neighborhood that the disease had been carried to the Weequahic section by the Italians. Since so far their neighborhood had reported the most cases of polio in the city and ours had reported none, it was believed that, true to their word, the Italians had driven across town that afternoon intending to infect the Jews with polio and that they had succeeded.

BUCKY CANTOR'S MOTHER had died in childbirth, and he had been raised by his maternal grandparents in a tenement housing twelve families on Barclay Street off lower Avon Avenue, in one of the poorer sections of the city. His father, from whom he'd inherited his bad eyesight, was a bookkeeper for a big downtown department store who had an inordinate fondness for betting on horses. Shortly after his wife's death and his son's birth he was convicted of larceny for stealing from his employer to cover his gambling debts—it turned out he'd been lining his pockets from the day he'd taken the job. He served two years in jail and, after his release, never returned to Newark. Instead of having a father, the boy, whose given name was Eugene, took his instruction in life from the big, bear-like, hardworking grandfather in whose Avon Avenue grocery store he worked after school and on Saturdays. He was five when his father married for a second time and hired a lawyer to get the boy to come to live with him and his new wife down in Perth Amboy where he had a job in the shipyards. The grandfather, rather than going out to hire his own lawyer, drove straight to Perth Amboy, where there was a confrontation in which he was said to have threatened to break his one-time son-in-law's neck should he dare to try in any way to interfere in Eugene's life. After that, Eugene's father was never heard from again.

It was from heaving crates of produce around the store with his grandfather that he began to develop his chest and arms, and from running up and down the three flights to their flat innumerable times a day that he began to develop his legs. And it was from his grandfather's intrepidness that he learned how to pit himself against any obstacle, including having been born the son of a man his grandfather would describe for as long as he lived as "a very shady character." He wanted as a boy to be physically strong, just like his grandfather, and not to have to wear thick glasses. But his eyes were so bad that when he put the glasses away at night to get ready for bed, he could barely make out the shape of the few pieces of furniture in his room. His grandfather, who had never given a second thought to his

own disadvantages, instructed the unhappy child—
when he'd first donned glasses at the age of eight—
that his eyes were now as good as anyone else's.
After that, there was nothing further to be said on
the subject.

His grandmother was a warm, tenderhearted little woman, a good, sound parental counterweight to
his grandfather. She bore hardship bravely, though
teared up whenever mention was made of the twenty-
year-old daughter who had died in childbirth. She
was much loved by the customers in the store, and
at home, where her hands were never still, she followed with half an ear *Life Can Be Beautiful* and the
other soap operas she liked where the listener is always shuddering, always nervous, at the prospect of
the next misfortune. In the few hours a day when
she was not assisting in the grocery, she devoted
herself wholeheartedly to Eugene's welfare, nursing
him through measles, mumps, and chickenpox, seeing that his clothes were always clean and mended,
that his homework was done, that his report cards
were signed, that he was taken to the dentist regularly (as few poor children were in those days), that
the food she cooked for him was hearty and plen-
tiful, and that his fees were paid at the synagogue

where he went after school for Hebrew classes to prepare for his bar mitzvah. But for the trio of common infectious childhood diseases, the boy had unwavering good health, strong even teeth, an overall sense of physical well-being that must have had something to do with the way she had mothered him, trying to do everything that was thought, in those days, to be good for a growing child. Between her and her husband there was rarely squabbling—each knew the job to do and how best to do it, and each carried it off with an avidity whose example was not lost on young Eugene.

The grandfather saw to the boy's masculine development, always on the alert to eradicate any weakness that might have been bequeathed—along with the poor eyesight—by his natural father and to teach the boy that a man's every endeavor was imbued with responsibility. His grandfather's dominance wasn't always easy to abide, but when Eugene met his expectations, the praise was never grudging. There was the time, when he was just ten, that the boy came upon a large gray rat in the dim stockroom back of the store. It was already dark outside when he saw the rat scuttling in and out of a stack of empty grocery cartons that he had helped his grandfather to unpack. His impulse was, of course, to run. Instead, knowing his grandfather was out front with a customer, he reached noiselessly into a corner for the deep, heavy coal shovel with which he was learning how to tend the furnace that heated the store.

Holding his breath, he advanced on tiptoe until he had stalked the panicked rat into a corner. When the boy lifted the shovel into the air, the rat rose on its hind legs and gnashed its frightening teeth, deploying itself to spring. But before it could leave the floor, he brought the underside of the shovel swiftly downward and, catching the rodent squarely on the skull, smashed its head open. Blood intermingled with bits of bone and brain drained into the cracks of the stockroom floorboards as—having failed to suppress completely a sudden impulse to vomit—he used the shovel blade to scoop up the dead animal. It was heavy, heavier than he could have imagined, and looked larger and longer resting in the shovel than it had up on its hind legs. Strangely, nothing—not even the lifeless strand of tail and the four motionless feet—looked quite as dead as the pairs of needle-thin, bloodstained whiskers. With his weapon raised over his head, he had not registered the whiskers; he had not registered anything other than the words "Kill it!" as if they were being formulated in his brain by his grandfather. He waited until the customer had left with her grocery bag and then, holding the shovel straight out in front of him—and poker-faced to reveal how unfazed he was—he carried the dead rat through to the front of the store to display to his grandfather before continuing out the door. At the corner, jiggling the carcass free of the shovel, he poked it through the iron grate into the flowing sewer. He returned to the store and, with a scrub brush, brown soap, rags, and a bucket of water, cleaned the floor of his vomit and the traces of the rat and rinsed off the shovel.

It was following this triumph that his grandfather—because of the nickname's connotation of obstinacy and gutsy, spirited, strong-willed fortitude—took to calling the bespectacled ten-year-old Bucky.

The grandfather, Sam Cantor, had come alone to America in the 1880s as an immigrant child from

a Jewish village in Polish Galicia. His fearlessness
had been learned in the Newark streets, where his
nose had been broken more than once in fights
with anti-Semitic gangs. The violent aggression
against Jews that was commonplace in the city during his slum boyhood did much to form his view of
life and his grandson's view in turn. He encouraged
the grandson to stand up for himself as a man and
to stand up for himself as a Jew, and to understand
that one's battles were never over and that, in the
relentless skirmish that living is, "when you have to
pay the price, you pay it." The broken nose in the
middle of his grandfather's face had always testified
to the boy that though the world had tried, it could
not crush him. The old man was dead of a heart attack by July 1944, when the ten Italians drove up
to the playground and single-handedly Mr. Cantor
turned them back, but that didn't mean he wasn't
there throughout the confrontation.

A boy who'd lost a mother at birth and a father
to jail, a boy whose parents figured not at all in his
earliest recollections, couldn't have been more fortunate in the surrogates he'd inherited to make
him strong in every way—he'd only rarely allow

the thought of his missing parents to torment him, even if his biography had been determined by their absence.

MR. CANTOR had been twenty and a college junior when the U.S. Pacific Fleet was bombed and nearly destroyed in the surprise Japanese attack at Pearl Harbor on Sunday, December 7, 1941. On Monday the eighth he went off to the recruiting station outside City Hall to join the fight. But because of his eyes nobody would have him, not the army, the navy, the coast guard, or the marines. He was classified 4-F and sent back to Panzer College to continue preparing to be a phys ed teacher. His grandfather had only recently died, and however irrational the thought, Mr. Cantor felt as though he had let him down and failed to meet the expectations of his undeflectable mentor. What good were his muscular build and his athletic prowess if he couldn't exploit them as a soldier? He hadn't been lifting weights since early adolescence merely to be strong enough to hurl the javelin—he had made himself strong enough to be a marine.

After America entered the war, he was still walking the streets while all the able-bodied men his age were off training to fight the Japs and the Germans, among them his two closest friends from Panzer, who'd lined up outside the recruiting station with him on the morning of December 8. His grandmother, with whom he still lived while commuting to Panzer, heard him weeping in his bedroom the night his buddies Dave and Jake went off to Fort Dix to begin basic training without him, heard him weeping as she'd never known Eugene to weep before. He was ashamed to be seen in civilian clothes, ashamed when he watched the newsreels of the war at the movies, ashamed when he took the bus home to Newark from East Orange at the end of the school day and sat beside someone reading in the evening paper the day's biggest story: "Bataan Falls," "Corregidor Falls," "Wake Island Falls." He felt the shame of someone who might by himself have made a difference as the U.S. forces in the Pacific suffered one colossal defeat after another.

Because of the war and the draft, jobs in the school system for male gym teachers were so numerous that even before he graduated from Panzer in June of 1943, he had nailed down a position at ten-year-old Chancellor Avenue School and signed on as the summertime playground director. His goal was to teach phys ed and coach at Weequahic, the high school that had opened next door to Chancellor. It was because both schools had overwhelmingly Jewish student bodies and excellent scholastic credentials that Mr. Cantor was drawn to them. He wanted to teach these kids to excel in sports as well as in their studies and to value sportsmanship and what could be learned through competition on a playing field. He wanted to teach them what his grandfather had taught him: toughness and determination, to be physically brave and physically fit and never to allow themselves to be pushed around or, just because they knew how to use their brains, to be defamed as Jewish weaklings and sissies.

THE NEWS THAT SWEPT the playground after Herbie Steinmark and Alan Michaels were transported by ambulance to the isolation ward at Beth Israel Hospital was that they were both completely paralyzed and, no longer able to breathe on their own, were being kept alive in iron lungs. Though not everybody had shown up at the playground that morning, there were still enough kids for four teams to be organized for their daylong round robin of five-inning games. Mr. Cantor estimated that altogether, in addition to Herbie and Alan, some fifteen or twenty of the ninety or so playground regulars were missing—kept home, he assumed, by their parents because of the polio scare. Knowing as he did the protectiveness of the Jewish parents in the neighborhood and the maternal concern of the watchful mothers, he was in fact surprised that a good many more hadn't wound up staying away. Probably he had done some good by speaking to them as he had the day before.

"Boys," he had said, gathering them together on the field before they disbanded for dinner, "I don't want you to begin to panic. Polio is a disease that we have to live with every summer. It's a serious disease that's been around all my life. The best way to deal with the threat of polio is to stay healthy and strong. Try to wash yourself thoroughly every day and to eat right and to get eight hours of sleep and to drink eight glasses of water a day and not to give in to your worries and fears. We all want Herbie and Alan to get better as soon as possible. We all wish this hadn't happened to them. They're two terrific boys, and many of you are their close friends. Nevertheless, while they are recovering in the hospital, the rest of us have to go on living our lives. That means coming here to the playground every day and participating in sports as you always do. If any of you feel ill, of course you must tell your parents and stay at home and look after yourself until you've seen a doctor and are well. But if you're feeling fine, there's no reason in the world why you can't be as active as you like all summer long."

From the kitchen phone that evening he tried several times to call the Steinmark and Michaels families to express his concern and the concern of the boys at the playground and to find out more about the condition of the two sick boys. But there was no answer at either house. Not a good sign. The families must still have been at the hospital at nine-fifteen at night.

Then the phone rang. It was Marcia, calling from the Poconos. She had heard about the two kids at his playground. "I spoke to my folks. They told me. Are you all right?"

"I'm fine," he said, extending the cord of the phone so he could stand where it was a touch cooler, closer to the screen of the open window. "All the other boys are fine. I've been trying to reach the families of the boys in the hospital to find out how they're doing."

"I miss you," Marcia said, "and I worry about you."

"I miss you too," he said, "but there's nothing to worry about."

"Now I'm sorry I came up here." She was working for the second summer as a head counselor at Indian Hill, a camp for Jewish boys and girls in Pennsylvania's Pocono Mountains seventy miles from the city; during the year she was a first-grade teacher at Chancellor—they'd met as new faculty members the previous fall. "It sounds awful," she said.

"It's awful for the two boys and their families," he said, "but the situation is far from out of hand. You shouldn't think it is."

"My mother said something about the Italians coming up to the playground to spread it."

"The Italians didn't spread anything. I was there. I know what happened. They were a bunch of wiseguys, that's all. They spit all over the street, and we washed it away. Polio is polio—nobody knows how it spreads. Summer comes and there it is, and there's nothing much you can do."

"I love you, Bucky. I think of you constantly."

Discreetly, so none of the neighbors could hear him through the open window, he lowered his voice and replied, "I love you too." It was difficult to tell her that because he had disciplined himself—sensibly, he thought—not to pine for her too much while she was away. It was also difficult because he'd never declared himself that openly to another girl and still found the words awkward to say.

"I have to get off the phone," Marcia said. "There's somebody waiting behind me. Please take care of yourself."

"I do. I will. But don't worry. Don't be frightened. There's nothing to be frightened about."

The next day, news raced through the community that within the Weequahic school district there were eleven new cases of polio—as many as had been reported there in the previous three years combined, and it was still only July, with a good two months to go before the polio season was over. Eleven new cases, and during the night Alan Michaels, Mr. Cantor's favorite, had died. The disease had finished him off in seventy-two hours.

The day following was Saturday, and the playground was open to organized activities only until noon, when the rising and falling whine of the air-raid sirens sounded in their weekly test from utility poles across the city. Instead of going back to Barclay Street after closing up, to help his grandmother with the week's grocery shopping—the stock of their own grocery store had been sold for a pittance after his grandfather's death—he showered in the boys' locker room and put on a clean shirt and trousers and a pair of polished shoes that he'd brought with him in a paper bag. Then he walked the length of Chancellor Avenue, all the way down the hill to Fabyan Place, where Alan Michaels's family lived. Despite polio's striking in the neighborhood, the store-lined main street was full of people out doing their Saturday grocery shopping and picking up their dry-cleaning and their drug prescriptions and whatever they needed from the electrical shop and the ladies' wear shop and the optical shop and the hardware store. In Frenchy's barber shop every seat was occupied by one of the neighborhood men waiting to get a haircut or a shave; in the shoe repair shop next door, the Italian shopkeeper—the street's only non-Jewish shop owner, not excluding Frenchy—was busy finding people's finished shoes in a pile of them on his cluttered counter while the

Italian radio station blared through his open doorway. Already the stores had their front awnings rolled down to keep the sun from beaming hotly through the plate-glass window looking onto the street.

It was a bright, cloudless day and the temperature was rising by the hour. Boys from his gym classes and from the playground became excited when they spotted him out on Chancellor Avenue— since he lived not in the neighborhood but down in the South Side school district, they were used to seeing him only in his official capacities as gym teacher and playground director. He waved when they called "Mr. Cantor!" and he smiled and nodded at their parents, some of whom he recognized from PTA meetings. One of the fathers stopped to talk to him. "I want to shake your hand, young man," he said to Mr. Cantor. "You told those dagos where to get off. Those dirty dogs. One against ten. You're a brave young man." "Thank you, sir." "I'm Murray Rosenfield. I'm Joey's father." "Thank you, Mr. Rosenfield." Next, a woman who was out shopping stopped to speak to him. She smiled politely and said, "I'm Mrs. Lewy. I'm Bernie's mother. My son worships you, Mr. Cantor. But I have one thing to ask you. With what's going on in the city, do you think the boys should be running around in heat like this? Bernie comes home soaked to the skin. Is that a good idea? Look at what's happened to Alan. How does a family recover from something like this? His two brothers away in the war, and now this." "I don't let the boys overexert themselves, Mrs. Lewy. I watch out for them." "Bernie," she said, "doesn't know when to quit. He can run all day and all night if somebody doesn't stop him." "I'll be sure to stop him if he gets too hot. I'll keep my eye on him." "Oh, thank you, thank you. Everybody is very happy that it's you who's looking after the boys." "I hope I'm helping," Mr. Cantor replied. A small crowd had gathered while he'd been talking to Bernie's mother, and now a second woman approached and reached for his sleeve to get his attention. "And where's the Board of Health in all this?" "Are you asking me?" Mr. Cantor said. "Yes, you. Eleven new cases in the Weequahic section overnight! One child dead! I want to know what the Board of Health is doing to protect our children." "I don't work for the Board of Health," he replied. "I'm playground director at Chancellor." "Somebody said you were with the Board of

Health," she charged him. "No, I'm not. I wish I could help you but I'm attached to the schools." "You dial the Board of Health," she said, "and you get a busy signal. I think they purposely leave the phone off the hook." "The Board of Health was here," another woman put in. "I saw them. They put a quarantine sign up on a house on my street." Her voice full of distress, she said, "There's a case of polio on my street!" "And the Board of Health does nothing!" someone else said angrily. "What is the city doing to stop this? Nothing!" "There's got to be something to do—but they're not doing it!" "They should inspect the milk that kids drink—polio comes from dirty cows and their infected milk." "No," said someone else, "it isn't the cows—it's the bottles. They don't sterilize those milk bottles right." "Why don't they fumigate?" another voice said. "Why don't they use disinfectant? Disinfect *everything*." "Why don't they do like they did when I was a child? They tied camphor balls around our necks. They had something that stunk bad they used to call asafetida—maybe that would work now." "Why don't they spread some kind of chemical on the streets and kill it that way?" "Forget about chemicals," someone else said. "The most important thing is for the children to wash their hands. Constantly wash their hands. Cleanliness! Cleanliness is the only cure!" "And another important thing," Mr. Cantor put in, "is for all of you to calm down and not lose your self-control and panic. And not communicate panic to the children. The important thing is to keep everything in their lives as normal as possible and for you all, in what you say to them, to try to stay reasonable and calm." "Wouldn't it be better if they stayed home till this passes over?" another woman said to him. "Isn't home the safest place in a crisis like this? I'm Richie Tulin's mother. Richie is crazy about you, Mr. Cantor. All the boys are. But wouldn't Richie be better off, wouldn't all the boys be better off, if you closed down the playground and they stayed at home?" "Shutting down the playground isn't up to me, Mrs. Tulin. That would be up to the superintendent of schools." "Don't think I'm blaming you for what's happening," she said. "No, no, I know you're not. You're a mother. You're concerned. I understand everyone's concern." "Our Jewish children are our riches," someone said. "Why is it attacking our beautiful Jewish children?" "I'm not a doctor. I'm not a scientist. I don't know why it attacks who it attacks. I don't believe that anyone does. That's why everybody tries to find who or what is guilty. They try to figure out what's responsible so they can eliminate it." "But what about the Italians? It had to be the Italians!" "No, no, I don't think so. I was there when the Italians came. They had no contact with the children. It was not the Italians. Look, you mustn't be eaten up with worry and you mustn't be eaten up with fear. What's important is not to infect the children with the germ of fear. We'll come through this, believe me. We'll all do our bit and stay calm and do everything we can to protect the children, and we'll all come through this together," he said. "Oh, thank you, young man. You're a splendid young man." "I have to be going, you'll have to excuse me," he told them all, looking one last time into their anxious eyes, beseeching him as though he were something far more powerful than a playground director twenty-three years old.

FABYAN PLACE was the last street in Newark before the railroad tracks and the lumberyards and the border with Irvington. Like the other residential streets that branched off Chancellor, it was lined

with two-and-a-half-story frame houses fronted by
red-brick stoops and hedged-in tiny yards and separated from one another by narrow cement driveways and small garages. At the curb in front of each
stoop was a young shade tree planted in the last
decade by the city and looking parched now after
weeks of torrid temperatures and no rain. Nothing
about the clean and quiet street gave evidence of
unhealthiness or infection. In every house on every
floor either the shades were pulled or the drapes
drawn to keep out the ferocious heat. There was
no one to be seen anywhere, and Mr. Cantor wondered if it was because of the heat or because the
neighbors were keeping their children indoors out
of respect for the Michaels family—or perhaps out
of terror of the Michaels family.

Then a figure emerged from around the Lyons
Avenue corner, making its solitary way through the
brilliant light burning down on Fabyan Place and
already softening the asphalt street. Mr. Cantor
recognized who it was, even from afar, by the pe-
culiar walk. It was Horace. Every man, woman, and
child in the Weequahic section recognized Horace,
largely because it was always so disquieting to find
him heading one's way. When the smaller children

saw him they ran to the other side of the street; when adults saw him they lowered their eyes. Horace was the neighborhood's "moron," a skinny man in his thirties or forties—no one knew his age for sure—whose mental development had stopped at around six and whom a psychologist would likely have categorized as an imbecile, or even an idiot, rather than the moron he'd been unclinically dubbed years before by the neighborhood youngsters. He dragged his feet beneath him, and his head, jutting forward from his neck like a turtle's, bobbed loosely with each step, so that altogether he appeared to be not so much walking as staggering forward. Spittle gathered at the corners of his mouth on the rare occasions when he spoke, and when he was silent he would sometimes drool. He had a thin, irregular face that looked as if it had been crushed and twisted in the vise of the birth canal, except for his nose, which was big and, given the narrowness of his face, oddly and grotesquely bulbous, and which inspired some of the kids to taunt him by shouting "Hey, bugle nose!" when he shuffled by the stoop or the driveway where they were congregated. His clothing gave off a sour

smell regardless of the season, and his face was dotted with blood spots, tiny nicks in his skin certify-
ing that though Horace might have the mind of a
baby, he also had the beard of a man and, however
hazardously, shaved himself, or was shaved by one
of his parents, before he went out every day. Minutes earlier he must have left the little apartment
back of the tailor shop around the corner where he
lived with his parents, an aged couple who spoke
Yiddish to each other and heavily accented English
to the customers in the shop and were said to have
other, normal children who were grown and lived
elsewhere—amazingly enough, one of Horace's two
brothers was said to be a doctor and the other a
successful businessman. Horace was the family's
youngest, and he was out walking the neighborhood streets every day of the year, in the worst of
summer as in the worst of winter, when he wore an
oversized mackinaw with its hood pulled up over
his earmuffs and black galoshes with the toggles
undone and mittens for his large hands that were
attached to the cuffs of his sleeves with safety pins
and that dangled there unused no matter what the
temperature. It was an outfit in which, trudging

along, he looked even more outlandish than he did ordinarily making the rounds of the neighborhood alone.

Mr. Cantor found the Michaels house on the far side of the street, climbed the stoop steps, and, in the small hallway with the mailboxes, pushed the bell to their second-floor flat and heard it ringing upstairs. Slowly someone descended the interior stairs and opened the frosted glass door at the foot of the stairwell. The man who stood there was large and heavyset, and the buttons on his short-sleeved shirt pulled tightly across his belly. He had grainy dark patches under his eyes, and when he saw Mr. Cantor he was silent, as though grief had left him too stupefied to speak.

"I'm Bucky Cantor. I'm the playground director at Chancellor and a phys ed teacher there. Alan was in one of my gym classes. He was one of the boys who played ball up at the playground. I heard what happened and came to offer my condolences."

The man was a long time answering. "Alan talked about you," he finally said.

"Alan was a natural athlete. Alan was a very thoughtful boy. This is terrible, shocking news. It's incomprehensible. I came to tell you how upset I am for all of you."

It was very hot in the hallway, and both the men were perspiring heavily.

"Come upstairs," Mr. Michaels said. "We'll give you something cold."

"I don't want to bother you," Mr. Cantor replied. "I wanted to express my condolences and tell you what a fine boy you had for a son. He was a grownup in every way."

"There's iced tea. My sister-in-law made some. We had to call the doctor for my wife. She's been in bed since it happened. They had to give her pheno-barb. Come and have some iced tea."

"I don't want to intrude."

"Come. Alan told us all about Mr. Cantor and his muscles. He loved the playground." Then, his voice breaking, he said, "He loved life."

Mr. Cantor followed the large, grief-stricken man up the stairs and into the flat. All the shades were lowered and no lights were on. There was a console radio beside the sofa and two big soft club chairs opposite that. Mr. Cantor sat on the sofa while Mr. Michaels went to the kitchen and re-

turned with a glass of iced tea for the guest. He mo-
tioned for Mr. Cantor to sit closer to him in one of
the club chairs and then, sighing audibly, painfully,
he sat in the other chair, which had an ottoman at
its foot. Once he was stretched out across the ottoman and the chair, he looked as though he too,
like his wife, were in bed, drugged and incapable
of moving. Shock had rendered his face expression-
less. In the near darkness, the stained skin beneath
his eyes looked black, as if it had been imprinted in
ink with twin symbols of mourning. Ancient Jewish
death rites call for the rending of one's garments on
learning of the death of a loved one—Mr. Michaels
had affixed two dark patches to his colorless face
instead.

"We have sons in the army," he said, speaking
softly so no one in another room could hear, and
slowly, as if out of great fatigue. "Ever since they've
been overseas, not a day has gone by when I haven't
expected to hear the worst. So far they have survived the worst fighting, and yet their baby brother
wakes up a few mornings back with a stiff neck and
a high fever, and three days later he's gone. How
are we going to tell his brothers? How are we going
to write this to them in combat? A twelve-year-old

youngster, the best boy you could want, and he's gone. The first night he was so miserable that in the morning I thought that maybe the worst was over and the crisis had passed. But the worst had only begun. What a day that boy put in! The child was on fire. You read the thermometer and you couldn't believe it—a temperature of a hundred and six! As soon as the doctor came he immediately called the ambulance, and at the hospital they whisked him away from us—and that was it. We never saw our son alive again. He died all alone. No chance to say so much as goodbye. All we have of him is a closet with his clothes and his schoolbooks and his sports things, and there, over there, his fish."

For the first time, Mr. Cantor noticed the large glass aquarium up against the far wall, where not only were the shades drawn but dark drapes were pulled shut across a window that must have faced the driveway and the house next door. A neon light shone down on the tank, and inside he could see the population of tiny, many-hued fish, more than a dozen of them, either vanishing into a miniature grotto, green with miniature shrubbery, or sweeping the sandy bottom for food, or veering upward to suck at the surface, or just suspended stock-still near a silver cylinder bubbling air in one corner of the tank. Alan's handiwork, Mr. Cantor thought, a neatly outfitted habitat fastidiously managed and cared for.

"This morning," Mr. Michaels said, gesturing back over his shoulder at the tank, "I remembered to feed them. I jumped up in bed and remembered."

"He was the best boy," Mr. Cantor said, leaning across the chair so he could be heard while keeping his voice low.

"Always did his schoolwork," Mr. Michaels said. "Always helped his mother. Not a selfish bone in his body. Was going to begin in September to prepare for his bar mitzvah. Polite. Neat. Wrote each of his brothers V-mail letters every single week, letters full of news that he read to us at the dinner table. Always cheering his mother up when she would get down in the dumps about the two older boys. Always making her laugh. Even when he was a small boy you could have a good time laughing with Alan. Our house was where all their friends came to have a good time. The place was always full of boys. Why did Alan get polio? Why did he have to get sick and die?"

Mr. Cantor clutched the cold glass of iced tea in his hand without drinking from it, without even realizing he was holding it.

"All his friends are terrified," Mr. Michaels said. "They're terrified that they caught it from him and now they are going to get polio too. Their parents are hysterical. Nobody knows what to do. What is there to do? What should we have done? I rack my brain. Can there be a cleaner household than this one? Can there be a woman who keeps a more spotless house than my wife? Could there be a mother more attentive to her children's welfare? Could there be a boy who looked after his room and his clothes and himself any better than Alan did? Everything he did, he did it right the first time. And always happy. Always with a joke. So why did he die? Where is the fairness in that?"

"There is none," Mr. Cantor said.

"You do only the right thing, the right thing and the right thing and the right thing, going back all the way. You try to be a thoughtful person, a reasonable person, an accommodating person, and then this happens. Where is the sense in life?"

"It doesn't seem to have any," Mr. Cantor answered.

"Where are the scales of justice?" the poor man asked.

"I don't know, Mr. Michaels."

"Why does tragedy always strike down the people who least deserve it?"

"I don't know the answer," Mr. Cantor replied.

"Why not me instead of him?"

Mr. Cantor had no response at all to such a question. He could only shrug.

"A boy—tragedy strikes a *boy*. The cruelty of it!" Mr. Michaels said, pounding the arm of his chair with his open hand. "The meaninglessness of it! A terrible disease drops from the sky and somebody is dead overnight. A child, no less!"

Mr. Cantor wished that he knew a single word to utter that would alleviate, if only for a moment, the father's anguished suffering. But all he could do was nod his head.

"The other evening we were sitting outside," Mr. Michaels said. "Alan was with us. He had come back from tending his plot in the victory garden. He did that religiously. Last year we actually ate Alan's vegetables that he raised all summer long. A breeze came up. Unexpectedly it got breezy. Do you

remember, the other night? Around eight o'clock,
how refreshing it seemed?"

"Yes," Mr. Cantor said, but he hadn't been listening. He'd been looking across the room at the tropical fish swimming in the aquarium and thinking
that without Alan to tend them, they would starve
to death or be given away or, in time, be flushed
down the toilet by somebody in tears.

"It seemed like a blessing after the broiling day
we'd had. You wait and wait for a breeze. You think
a breeze will bring some relief. But you know what
I think it did instead?" Mr. Michaels asked. "I think
that breeze blew the polio germs around in the air,
around and around, the way you see leaves blow
around in a flurry. I think Alan was sitting there
and breathed in the germs from the breeze . . ." He
couldn't continue; he had begun to cry, awkwardly,
inexpertly, the way men cry who ordinarily like to
think of themselves as a match for anything.

Here a woman came out of a back bedroom; it
was the sister-in-law who was looking after Mrs.
Michaels. She stepped gently with her shoes on the
floor, as though inside the bedroom a restless child
had finally fallen asleep.

Quietly she said, "She wants to know who you're talking to."

"This is Mr. Cantor," said Mr. Michaels, wiping his eyes. "He is a teacher from Alan's school. How is she?" he asked his sister-in-law.

"Not good," she reported in a low voice. "It's the same story. 'Not my baby, not my baby.'"

"I'll be right in," he said.

"I should be going," Mr. Cantor said and got up from his chair and set the untouched iced tea down on a side table. "I only wanted to pay my respects. May I ask when the funeral is?"

"Tomorrow at ten. Schley Street Synagogue. Alan was the rabbi's Hebrew school favorite. He was *everybody's* favorite. Rabbi Slavin himself came here and offered the shul as soon as he heard what had happened. As a special honor to Alan. Everybody in the world loved that boy. He was one in a million."

"What did you teach him?" the sister-in-law asked Mr. Cantor.

"Gym."

"Anything with sports in it, Alan loved," she said. "And what a student. The apple of everyone's eye."

"I know that," said Mr. Cantor. "I see that. I can't express to you how very sorry I am."

Downstairs, as he stepped out onto the stoop, a woman rushed out of the first-floor flat and, excitedly taking him by his arm, asked, "Where is the quarantine sign? People have been coming and going from upstairs, in and out, in and out, and why isn't there a quarantine sign? I have small children. Why isn't there a quarantine sign protecting my children? Are you a patrolman from the Sanitary Squad?"

"I don't know anything about the Sanitary Squad. I'm from the playground. I teach at the school."

"Who is in charge then?" A small, dark woman laden with fear, her face contorted with emotion, she looked as if her life had already been wrecked by polio rather than by her children's having to live precariously within its reach. She looked no better than Mr. Michaels did.

"I suppose the Board of Health is in charge," Mr. Cantor said.

"Where are they?" she pleaded. "Where is somebody who is in charge! People on the street won't even walk in front of our house—they walk deliberately on the other side. The child is already dead," she added, incoherent now with desperation, "and still I'm waiting for a quarantine sign!" And here she let out a shriek. Mr. Cantor had never heard a shriek before, other than in a horror movie. It was different from a scream. It could have been generated by an electrical current. It was a high-pitched, protracted sound unlike any human noise he knew, and the eerie shock of it caused his skin to crawl.

HE'D HAD NO LUNCH, so he made his way to Syd's to get a hot dog. He was careful to walk on the shady side of the street, across from where nothing was sheltered from the glare of the sun and where he thought he could see heat waves shimmering above the sidewalk. Most of the shoppers had disappeared. It was one of those overpowering summer days when the thermometer registered an astonishing one hundred degrees and when, if the playground were open, he would have curtailed the softball games and encouraged the kids to use the chess- and checkerboards and the Ping-Pong tables set up in the shadow of the school. A lot of the boys took salt tablets that their mothers had given them for the heat, and wanted to go on play-

ing no matter how high the temperature soared,
even when the field's asphalt surface began to feel
spongy and to radiate heat under their sneakers and
the sun was so hot that you would think that rather
than darkening your bare skin it would bleach
you of all color before cremating you on the spot.
Fresh from hearing Alan's father's lamentation, Mr.
Cantor wondered if for the rest of the summer he
oughtn't to shut down all sports when the temperature hit ninety. That way, he'd at least be doing
something, though whether it was something that
would make any difference to the spread of polio,
he had no idea.

Syd's was almost empty. Somebody was cursing
at the pinball machine in the gloom at the back
of the store, and two high school boys he did not
know were goofing around by the jukebox, which
was playing "I'll Be Seeing You," one of the summer's favorites. It was a song that Marcia liked to
hear on the radio and that was as popular as it was
because of all the wives and girlfriends left behind
when their husbands and boyfriends went off for
the duration of the war. He remembered now that
he and Marcia had danced to the song on her back
porch during the week before she'd left for Indian

Hill. Dancing slowly together in a shuffling embrace while listening to "I'll Be Seeing You" had made them start to long for each other even before Marcia was gone.

There was no one sitting in any of the booths and nobody on any of the counter stools when Bucky took a seat adjacent to the screen door and the long serving window that opened onto Chancellor Avenue, in the path of whatever air might drift in from the street. A big fan was going at either end of the counter, but they didn't seem to do much good. The place was hot and the smell pervasive of french fries deep-frying in fat.

He got a hot dog and a frosted root beer and began to eat at the counter by himself. Out the window, across the way, trudging slowly up the hill in the annihilating heat of equatorial Newark, there was Horace again, no doubt headed to the playground, not understanding that today was Saturday and that, in the summer, the playground closed on Saturdays at noon. (It was not clear whether he understood what "summer," "playground," "closed," or "noon" was either, just as his failure to cross to the other side of the street probably meant that he could not perform the rudimentary thinking to conceptualize "shade" or even just seek it out instinctively, as any dog would on a day like this.) When Horace found none of the kids back of the school, what would he do next? Sit for hours on the bleachers waiting for them to turn up, or resume those neighborhood wanderings that made him look like someone out sleepwalking in the middle of the day? Yes, Alan was dead and polio a threat to the lives of all the city's children, and yet Mr. Cantor couldn't but find something dispiriting about watching Horace walk the streets by himself beneath the ferocity of that sun, isolated and brainless in a blazing world.

When the boys were playing ball Horace would either seat himself silently at the end of the bench where the team at bat was sitting or else get up and perambulate the field, stopping a foot or two away from one of the players in the field and remain there without moving. This went on all the time, and everybody knew that the only way a fielder could get rid of Horace—and get back to concentrating on the game—was to shake the moron's lifeless hand and say to him, "How ya doin', Horace?" Whereupon Horace would appear to be satisfied and head off to stand beside another of the players. All he asked of life was that—to have his hand shaken. None of the playground boys ever laughed at him or teased him—at least not when Mr. Cantor was around—except for the uncontrollably energetic Kopfermans, Myron and Danny. They were strong, burly boys, good at sports, Myron the overexcitable, belligerent one and Danny the mischievous, secretive one. The older one especially, eleven-year-old Myron, had all the makings of a bully and had to be reined in when there was a disagreement among the boys on the field or when he interfered with the girls jumping rope. Mr. Cantor spent no small portion of his time trying to inculcate in untamed Myron the spirit of fair play and also to caution him to refrain from pestering Horace.

"Look," Myron would say, "look, Horace. Look what I'm doing." When Horace saw the tip of Myron's sneaker beating rhythmically up and down on the bleacher step, his fingers would begin to twitch and his face would grow bright red and soon he would be waving his arms in the air as if he were fighting off a swarm of bees. More than once that summer Mr. Cantor had to tell Myron Kopferman to cut it out and not do it again. "Do what?

Do what?" Myron asked, managing to mask none of his insolence with a wide grin. "I'm tapping my foot, Mr. Cantor—don't I have a right to tap my foot?" "Knock it off, Myron," Mr. Cantor replied. The ten-year-old Kopferman boy, Danny, had a cap gun made of metal and modeled to look like a real revolver which he carried in his pocket, even when he was in the field playing second base. The cap gun produced a small explosive sound and smoke when the trigger was pressed. Danny liked to come up behind the other boys and try to frighten them with it. Mr. Cantor tolerated these hijinks only because the other boys were never really frightened. But one day Danny took out the toy weapon and waved it at Horace and told him to stick his hands in the air, which Horace did not do, and so Danny gleefully fired off five rounds of caps. The noise and smoke set Horace to howling, and in his clumsy, splayfooted way, he went running from his playground tormentor. Mr. Cantor confiscated the gun, and after that kept it in a drawer in his office, along with the toy "sheriff's" handcuffs that Danny had employed earlier in the summer to scare the playground's younger kids. Not for the first time he sent Danny Kopferman home for the day with a note telling his mother what her younger son had gotten up to. He doubted that she'd ever seen it.

Yushy, the guy in the mustard-smeared apron who'd been working for years behind the counter at Syd's, said to Mr. Cantor, "It's dead around here."

"It's hot," Mr. Cantor answered. "It's summer. It's the weekend. Everybody's down the shore or staying indoors."

"No, nobody's coming in because of that kid."

"Alan Michaels."

"Yeah," Yushy said. "He ate a hot dog here, and he went home and got polio and died, and now everybody's afraid to come in. It's bullshit. You don't get polio from a hot dog. We sell thousands of hot dogs and nobody gets polio. Then one kid gets polio and everybody says, 'It's the hot dogs at Syd's, it's the hot dogs at Syd's!' A boiled hot dog—how do you get polio from a boiled hot dog?"

"People are frightened," Mr. Cantor said. "They're scared to death, so they worry about everything."

"It's the wop bastards that brought it around," Yushy said.

"That's not likely," Mr. Cantor said.

"They did. They spit all over the place."

"I was there. We washed the spit away with ammonia."

"You washed the spit away but you didn't wash the polio away. You can't wash the polio away. You can't see it. It gets in the air and you open your mouth and breathe it in and next thing you got the polio. It's got nothing to do with hot dogs."

Mr. Cantor offered no response and, while listening to the end of the familiar song playing on the jukebox—and suddenly missing Marcia—finished up eating.

> I'll be seeing you,
> In every lovely summer's day,
> In every thing that's light and gay,
> I'll always think of you that way . . .

"Suppose the kid had had an ice cream sundae at Halem's," Yushy said. "Would nobody eat ice cream sundaes at Halem's? Suppose he had chow mein up at the chinks'—would nobody go up to the chinks for chow mein?"

"Probably," Mr. Cantor said.

"And what about the other kid that died?" Yushy asked.

"What other kid?"

"The kid that died this morning."

"What kid died? Herbie Steinmark died?"

"Yeah. He didn't eat no hot dogs here."

"Are you sure he died? Who told you Herbie Steinmark died?"

"Somebody. Somebody came in just before and told me. A couple of guys told me."

Mr. Cantor paid Yushy for the food and then, despite the tremendous heat—and unafraid of the heat—ran from Syd's across Chancellor and back to the playground, where he raced down the stairs to the basement door, unlocked it, and headed for his office. There he picked up the telephone and dialed the number of Beth Israel Hospital, one of a list of emergency numbers on a card that was thumb-tacked to the notice board over his phone. Directly above it was another card, bearing a quotation he had written out in pen from Joseph Lee, the father of the playground movement, whom he'd read about at Panzer; it had been up there since the first day he arrived on the job. "Play for the adult is recreation, the renewal of life; play for the child is growth, the gaining of life." Tacked up beside that was a notice that had arrived in the mail just the day before from the head of the recreation department to all playground directors:

> In view of the danger to Newark children in the present outbreak of polio, please give very strict attention to the following. If you have not sufficient washroom supplies on hand, order them at once. Go over wash bowls, toilet bowls, floors and walls daily with disinfectant, and see that everything is immaculately clean. Toilet facilities must be thoroughly scrubbed throughout the premises under your supervision. Give the above your personal and unremitting attention as long as the present outbreak menaces the community.

When he got through to the hospital, he asked the operator for patient information and then asked for the condition of Herbert Steinmark. He was told that the patient was no longer in the hospital. "But he's in an iron lung," Mr. Cantor protested. "The patient is deceased," said the operator.

Deceased? What could that word have to do with plump, round, smiling Herbie? He was the least coordinated of all the boys at the playground, and the most ingratiating. He was always among the boys who helped him put out the equipment first thing in the morning. In gym class at Chancellor, he was hopeless on the pommel horse and the parallel bars and with the rings and the climbing rope, but because he tried hard and was persistently good-natured, Mr. Cantor had never given him lower than a B. Alan the natural athlete and Herbie the hopeless athlete, completely lacking physical agility— both had been playing on the field the day the Italians tried to invade the playground, and both were dead, polio fatalities at the age of twelve.

Mr. Cantor rushed down the basement hall to the washroom that was used by the playground boys and, at the mercy of his grief, with no idea what to do with his misery, he grabbed the janitor's mop, a bucket of water, and a gallon can of disinfectant and swabbed the entire tile floor, profusely sweating while he worked. Next he went into the girls' washroom, and vigorously, in a mad rage, he cleaned the floor there. Then, with his clothes and his hands reeking of disinfectant, he took the bus home.

THE NEXT MORNING, after shaving, showering, and eating breakfast, he repolished his good shoes, put on his suit, a white shirt, and the darker of his two ties, and took the bus to Schley Street. The synagogue was a low, dismal yellow-brick box of a building across the street from an overgrown lot that had been converted into a neighborhood victory garden, probably the one where Alan had taken diligent care of his own vegetable plot. Mr. Cantor could see a few women, wearing broad-brimmed straw hats for protection from the morning sun, bent over and weeding small patches of land adjacent to an advertising billboard. In front of the synagogue a row of cars was parked, one of them a black hearse, whose driver stood at the curb moving a cloth over the front fender. Inside the hearse Mr. Cantor could see the casket. It was impossible to believe that Alan was lying in that pale, plain pine box merely from having caught a summertime disease. That box from which you cannot force your way out. That box in which a twelve-year-old was twelve years old forever. The rest of us live and grow older by the day, but he remains twelve. Millions of years go by, and he is still twelve.

Mr. Cantor took his folded yarmulke out of his pants pocket, slipped it on his head, and went inside, where he found an empty seat near the back. He followed the prayers in the prayer book and joined the congregation in the recitations. Midway through, a woman's voice was heard to scream, "She fainted! Help!" Rabbi Slavin briefly stopped the service while someone, most likely a doctor, rushed along the aisle and up the stairs to the balcony, to tend to whoever had passed out in the women's section. The synagogue temperature must have been at least ninety by then, and highest probably in the balcony. No wonder somebody had fainted. If the service didn't soon come to an end, people would start fainting everywhere. Even Mr. Cantor felt a little woozy inside his one suit, a woolen suit made to be worn in the winter.

The seat next to him was empty. He kept wanting Alan to walk in and take it. He wanted Alan to walk in with his baseball mitt and sit down beside him and, as he regularly did at noon on the playground bleachers, eat the sandwich out of his lunch bag beside Mr. Cantor.

The eulogy was delivered by Alan's uncle, Isadore Michaels, whose pharmacy had stood for years on the corner of Wainwright and Chancellor and whom all the customers called Doc. He was a jovial-looking man, heavyset and dark-complexioned like Alan's father, with those same grainy patches under his eyes. He alone was speaking because no other family member felt able to control his emotions enough to do it. There were many people sobbing, and not only in the women's section.

"God blessed us with Alan Avram Michaels for twelve years," his uncle Isadore said, smiling bravely. "And He blessed me with a nephew who I loved like my own child from the day he was born. On his way home every day after school, Alan would always stop by the store and sit at the counter and order a chocolate malted. When he was first starting school he was the skinniest kid in the world, and the idea was to fatten him up. If I was free, I'd go over to the soda fountain and make the malted for him myself and add in extra malt to put some pounds on him. Once that ritual began, it went on year after year. How I would enjoy those after-school visits from my extraordinary nephew!"

Here he had to take a moment to collect himself.

"Alan," he resumed, "was an authority on tropical fish. He could talk like an expert about everything you do to take care of all the different kinds of tropical fish. There was nothing more thrilling than to visit the house and sit with Alan alongside his aquarium and have him explain to you every-

thing about each of the fish and how they had ba-
bies and so on. You could sit there with him for an
hour and he still wouldn't be finished telling you all
that he knew. You came away from being with Alan
and you had a smile on your face and your spirits
were lifted, and you'd learned something besides.
How did he do it? How did this child do all that he
did for all of us adults? What was Alan's special secret? It was to live every day of life, seeing the wonder in everything and taking delight in everything,
whether it was his after-school malted, or his tropical fish, or the sports in which he excelled, or contributing to the war effort in the victory garden, or
what he'd studied that day at school. Alan packed
more healthy fun into his twelve years than most
people get in a lifetime. And Alan gave more pleasure to others than most people give in a lifetime.
Alan's life is ended . . ."

Here he had to stop again, and when he continued it was with a husky voice and on the edge of
tears.

"Alan's life is ended," he repeated, "and yet, in
our sorrow, we should remember that while he lived
it, it was an endless life. Every day was endless for
Alan because of his curiosity. Every day was end-

less for Alan because of his geniality. He remained a happy child all of his life, and with everything the child did, he always gave it his all. There are fates far worse than that in this world."

Afterward, Mr. Cantor stood outside on the synagogue steps to pay his respects to Alan's family and to thank Alan's uncle for all he had said. Who would have imagined, watching him in his white coat at the drugstore, measuring out tablets for someone's prescription, how eloquent an orator Doc Michaels could be, especially while the people scattered throughout the congregation, upstairs and down, were openly wailing from the impact of his words? Mr. Cantor saw four boys from the playground exiting together from the service: the Spector boy, the Sobelsohn boy, the Taback boy, and the Finkelstein boy. They all wore ill-fitting suits and white shirts and ties and hard shoes, and perspiration streamed down their faces. It wasn't impossible that their greatest hardship that day was their being strangled in all that heat by a starched collar and a tie rather than their having their initial encounter with death. Still, they had dressed in their best clothes and come to the synagogue despite the weather, and Mr. Cantor walked up to them and took each by the shoulder and then reassuringly patted his back. "Alan would be glad you were here," he told them quietly. "It was very thoughtful of you to do this."

Then someone touched *him* on the back. "Who are you going with?"

"What?"

"There—" The person pointed to a car some way from the hearse. "There, go with the Beckermans," and he was pushed toward a Plymouth sedan parked down the curb.

It hadn't been his plan to go out to the cemetery. After the synagogue service, he intended to return to help his grandmother finish up the weekend chores. But he got into the car whose door was being held open for him and sat in the back seat beside a woman with a black-veiled hat who was fanning herself by waving a handkerchief in front of her face, whose powder was streaky with perspiration. In the driver's seat was a chunky little man in a dark suit whose nose was broken like his grandfather's and maybe for the same reason: anti-Semites. Seated alongside him was a plain, dark-haired girl of fifteen or sixteen, who was introduced as Alan's cousin Meryl. The elder Beckermans were Alan's aunt and uncle on his mother's side. Mr. Cantor introduced himself as one of Alan's teachers.

They had to sit in the hot car some ten minutes, waiting for the funeral cortege to form behind the hearse. Mr. Cantor tried to remember what Isadore Michaels had said in his eulogy about how Alan's life, while Alan lived it, had seemed to the boy to be endless, but invariably he wound up instead imagining Alan roasting like a piece of meat in his box.

They proceeded down Schley Street to Chancellor Avenue, where they made a left and began the slow trek up Chancellor, past Alan's uncle's pharmacy and toward the grade school and the high school at the top of the hill. There was hardly any other traffic—most of the stores were closed except for Tabatchnick's, catering to the Sunday morning smoked-fish trade, the corner candy stores that were selling the Sunday papers, and the bakery, selling coffee cake and bagels for Sunday breakfast. In his twelve years, Alan would have been out on this street a thousand times, heading back and forth to school and to the playground, going out to get something for his mother, meeting his friends at Halem's, walking all the way up and all the way down the hill to Weequahic Park to go fishing and ice-skating and rowing on the lake. Now he was riding down Chancellor Avenue for the last time, at the head of a funeral cortege and inside that box. If this car is an oven, Mr. Cantor thought, imagine the inside of that box.

Everyone in the car had been silent until they nearly reached the crest of the hill and were passing Syd's hot dog joint.

"Why did he have to eat in that filthy hole?" Mrs. Beckerman said. "Why couldn't he wait to get home and take something from the Frigidaire? Why do they allow that place to remain open across from a school? In summertime, no less."

"Edith," Mr. Beckerman said, "calm down."

"Ma," Alan's cousin Meryl said, "all the kids eat there. It's a hangout."

"It's a cesspool," Mrs. Beckerman said. "In polio season, for a boy with Alan's brains to go into a place like that, in this heat—"

"Enough, Edith. It's hot. We all know it's hot."

"There's his school," Mrs. Beckerman said as they reached the top of the hill and were passing the pale stone façade of the grade school where Mr. Cantor taught. "How many children love school the way Alan did? From the day he started, he loved it."

Perhaps the observation was being addressed to him, as a representative of the school. Mr. Cantor said, "He was an outstanding student."

"And there's Weequahic. He would have been an honor student at Weequahic. He was already planning to take Latin. Latin! I had a nickname for him. I called him Brilliant."

"That he was," Mr. Cantor said, thinking of Alan's father at the house and his uncle at the synagogue and now his aunt in the car—all of them gushing for the same good reason: because Alan deserved no less. They will lament to their graves losing this marvelous boy.

"In college," Mrs. Beckerman said, "he planned to study science. He wanted to be a scientist and cure disease. He read a book about Louis Pasteur and knew everything about how Louis Pasteur discovered that germs are invisible. He wanted to be another Louis Pasteur," she said, mapping out the whole of a future that was never to be. "Instead," she concluded, "he had to go to eat in a place *crawling* with germs."

"Edith, that's enough," Mr. Beckerman said. "We don't know how he got sick or where. Polio is all over the city. There's an epidemic. It's every place you look. He got a bad case and he died. That's all we know. Everything else is talk that gets you no-where. We don't know what his future would have been."

"We do!" she said angrily. "That child could have been anything!"

"Okay, you're right. I'm not arguing. Let's just get to the cemetery and give him a proper burial. That's all we can do for him now."

"And the two other boys," Mrs. Beckerman said. "God forbid anything should happen to them."

"They made it this far," Mr. Beckerman said, "they'll make it the rest of the way. The war will soon be over and Larry and Lenny will be safely home."

"And they'll never see their baby brother again. Alan will still be gone," she said. "There's no bring-ing him back."

"Edith," he said, "we *know* that. Edith, you're talking and you're not saying anything that every-body doesn't know."

"Let her speak, Daddy," Meryl said.

"But what good does it do," Mr. Beckerman asked, "going on and on?"

"It does good," the girl said. "It does her good."

"Thank you, darling," Mrs. Beckerman said.

All the windows were rolled down, but Mr. Cantor felt as though he were wrapped not in a suit but a blanket. The cortege had reached the park and turned right onto Elizabeth Avenue and was passing through Hillside and across the railroad overpass into Elizabeth, and he hoped that it wasn't much more time before they reached the cemetery. He imagined that if Alan lay roasting in that box for much longer, the box would somehow ignite and explode, and as though a hand grenade had gone off inside, the boy's remains would come bursting out all over the hearse and the street.

WHY DOES POLIO strike only in the summer? At the cemetery, standing there bareheaded but for his yarmulke, he had to wonder if polio couldn't be caused by the summer sun itself. At midday, in its full overhead onslaught, it seemed to have more than sufficient strength to cripple and kill, and to be rather more likely to do so than a microscopic germ in a hot dog.

A grave had been dug for Alan's casket. It was the second open grave Mr. Cantor had ever seen, the first having been his grandfather's, three years earlier, just before the war began. Then he'd been weighed down caring for his grandmother and holding her close to him throughout the cemetery service so that her legs didn't give way. After that, he'd been so busy looking after her and staying in every night with her and eventually getting her out once a week for a movie and an ice cream sundae that it was a while before he could find the time to contemplate all he himself had lost. But as Alan's casket was lowered into the ground—as Mrs. Michaels lunged for the grave, crying "No! Not my baby!"—death revealed itself to him no less powerfully than the incessant beating of the sun on his yarmulke'd head.

They all joined the rabbi in reciting the mourner's prayer, praising God's almightiness, praising extravagantly, unstintingly, the very God who allowed everything, including children, to be destroyed by death. Between the death of Alan Michaels and the communal recitation of the God-glorifying Kaddish, Alan's family had had an interlude of some twenty-four hours to hate and loathe God for what

He had inflicted upon them—not, of course, that it would have occurred to them to respond like that to Alan's death, and certainly not without fearing to incur God's wrath, prompting Him to wrest Larry and Lenny Michaels from them next.

But what might not have occurred to the Michaels family had not been lost on Mr. Cantor. To be sure, he himself hadn't dared to turn against God for taking his grandfather when the old man reached a timely age to die. But for killing Alan with polio at twelve? For the very existence of polio? How could there be forgiveness—let alone hallelujahs—in the face of such lunatic cruelty? It would have seemed far less of an affront to Mr. Cantor for the group gathered in mourning to declare themselves the celebrants of solar majesty, the children of an ever-constant solar deity, and, in the fervent way of our hemisphere's ancient heathen civilizations, to abandon themselves in a ritual sun dance around the dead boy's grave—better that, better to sanctify and placate the unrefracted rays of Great Father Sun than to submit to a supreme being for whatever atrocious crime it pleases Him to perpetrate. Yes, better by far to praise the irreplaceable generator that has sustained our existence from its beginning—better by far to honor in prayer one's tangible daily encounter with that ubiquitous eye of gold isolated in the blue body of the sky and its immanent power to incinerate the earth—than to swallow the official lie that God is good and truckle before a cold-blooded murderer of children. Better for one's dignity, for one's humanity, for one's worth altogether, not to mention for one's everyday idea of whatever the hell is going on here.

. . . Y'hei sh'mei raboh m'vorakh l'olam ul'olmei ol'mayoh.
    May His great Name be blessed forever and ever.
Yis'borakh v'yish'tabach v'yis'po'ar v'yis'romam v'yis'nasei
    Blessed, praised, glorified, exalted, extolled,
v'yis'hadar v'yis'aleh v'yis'halal sh'mei d'kud'shoh
    mighty, upraised, and lauded be the Name of the
    Holy One,
B'rikh hu . . .
    Blessed is He.

Four times during the prayer, at the grave of this child, the mourners repeated, "*Omein.*"

Only when the funeral cortege had left the sprawl of tombstones behind and was exiting between the gates onto McClellan Street did he suddenly remember the visits he used to make as a boy to the

Jewish cemetery on Grove Street where his mother, and now his grandfather, were buried and where his grandmother and he would be buried in turn. As a child he'd been taken by his grandparents to visit his mother's grave every year to commemorate her birthday in May, though from his first childhood visit on, he could not believe that she was interred there. Standing between his tearful grandparents, he always felt that he was going along with a game by pretending that she was—never more than at the cemetery did he feel that his having had a mother was a made-up story to begin with. And yet, despite his knowing that his annual visit was the queerest thing he was called upon to do, he would not ever refuse to go. If this was part of being a good son to a mother woven nowhere into his memories, then he did it, even when it felt like a hollow performance.

Whenever he tried at the graveside to summon up a thought appropriate to the occasion, he would remember the story his grandmother had told him about his mother and the fish. Of all her stories—standard inspirational stories about how clever Doris had been in school and how helpful she'd been around the house and how she'd loved as a child

to sit at the cash register in the store ringing up
the sales, just the way he did when he was small—
this was the one that had lodged in his mind. The
unforgotten event occurred on a spring afternoon
long before her death and his birth, when, to prepare for Passover, his grandmother would walk up
Avon Avenue to the fish store to choose two live
carp from the fishmonger's tank and bring them
home in a pail and keep them alive in the tin tub
that the family used for taking baths. She'd fill the
tub with water and leave the fish there until it was
time to chop off their heads and tails, scale them,
and cook them to make gefilte fish. One day when
Mr. Cantor's mother was five years old, she'd come
bounding up the stairs from kindergarten, found
the fish swimming in the tin tub, and after quickly
removing her clothes, got into the tub to play with
them. His grandmother found her there when she
came up from the store to fix her an after-school
snack. They never told his grandfather what the
child had done for fear that he might punish her
for it. Even when the little boy was told about the
fish by his grandmother—he was then himself in
kindergarten—he was cautioned to keep the story
a secret so as not to upset his grandfather, who, in

the first years after his cherished daughter's death, was able to deflect the anguish of losing her only by never speaking of her.

It may have seemed odd for Mr. Cantor to think of this story at his mother's graveside, but what else that was memorable was there to think about?

BY THE END of the next week, Weequahic had reported the summer's highest number of polio cases of any school district in the city. The playground itself was geographically ringed with new cases. Across from the playground on Hobson Street a ten-year-old girl, Lillian Sussman, had been stricken; across from the school on Bayview Avenue a six-year-old girl, Barbara Friedman, had been stricken—and neither was among the girls who jumped rope regularly at the playground, though there were now less than half as many of them around since the polio scare had begun. And down from the playground on Vassar Avenue, the two Kopferman brothers, Danny and Myron, had also been stricken. The evening of the day he heard the news about the Kopferman boys, he telephoned their house. He got Mrs. Kopferman. He explained who he was and why he was calling.

"You!" shouted Mrs. Kopferman. "You have the nerve to call?"

"Excuse me," Mr. Cantor said. "I don't understand."

"What don't you understand? You don't understand that in summertime you use your head with children running around in the heat? That you don't let them drink from the public fountain? That you watch when they are pouring sweat? Do you know how to use the eyes that God gave you and watch over children during polio season? No! Not for a minute!"

"Mrs. Kopferman, I assure you, I am careful with all the boys."

"So why do I have two paralyzed children? Both my boys! All that I've got! Explain that to me! You let them run around like animals up there—and you wonder why they get polio! Because of you! Because of a reckless, irresponsible idiot like you!" And she hung up.

He had called the Kopfermans from the kitchen, after he had sent his grandmother downstairs to sit outside with the neighbors and he had finished cleaning up from dinner. The day's heat had not broken, and indoors it was suffocatingly hot. When

he hung up from the phone call he was saturated
with perspiration, even though before eating he had
taken a shower and changed into fresh clothes. How
he wished his grandfather were around for him to
talk to. He knew that Mrs. Kopferman was hysterical; he knew that she was overcome with grief and
crazily lashing out at him; but he would have liked
to have his grandfather there to assure him that he
was not culpable in the ways she had said. This was
his first direct confrontation with vile accusation
and intemperate hatred, and it had unstrung him
far more than dealing with the ten menacing Italians at the playground.

It was seven o'clock and still bright outdoors
when he went three flights down the scuffed steps
of the outside wooden staircase to visit for a moment with the neighbors before he took a walk.
His grandmother was sitting with them in front of
the building, using a citronella candle to keep the
mosquitoes away. They sat on fold-up beach chairs
and were talking about polio. The older ones, like
his grandmother, had lived through the city's 1916
epidemic and were lamenting the fact that in the
intervening years science had been unable to find
a cure for the disease or come up with an idea of

how to prevent it. Look at Weequahic, they said, as clean and sanitary as any section in the city, and it's the worst hit. There was talk, somebody said, of keeping the colored cleaning women from coming to the neighborhood for fear that they carried the polio germs up from the slums. Somebody else said that in his estimation the disease was spread by money, by paper money passing from hand to hand. The important thing, he said, was always to wash your hands after you handled paper money or coins. What about the mail, someone else said, you don't think it could be spread by the mail? What are you going to do, somebody retorted, suspend delivering the mail? The whole city would come to a halt.

Six or seven weeks ago they would have been talking about the war news.

He heard a phone ringing and realized it was from their flat and that it must be Marcia calling from camp. Every school day for the past year they'd see each other at least once or twice in the corridors during school hours and then spend the weekends together, and this was the first extended period since they'd met that they were apart. He missed her, and he missed the Steinberg family, who had been kind and welcoming to him from the start. Her father was a doctor and her mother had formerly been a high school English teacher, and they lived, with Marcia's two younger sisters—twins in the sixth grade at Maple Avenue School—in a large, comfortable house on Goldsmith Avenue, a block up from Dr. Steinberg's Elizabeth Avenue office. After Mrs. Kopferman had accused Mr. Cantor of criminal negligence, he had thought about going to see Dr. Steinberg to talk to him about the epidemic and find out more about the disease. Dr. Steinberg was an educated man (in this way unlike the grandfather, who'd never read a book), and when he spoke Mr. Cantor always felt confident that he knew what he was talking about. He was no replacement for his grandfather—and no replacement, certainly, for a father of his own—but he was now the man he most admired and relied on. On his first date with Marcia, when he asked about her family, she had said of her father that he was not only wonderful with his patients but that he had a gift for keeping everybody in their household content and justly settling all her kid sisters' spats. He was the best judge of character she'd ever known. "My mother," she'd say, "calls him 'the impeccable thermometer of the family's emotional temperature.' There's no doctor I know of," she told him, "who's more humane than my dad."

"It's you!" Mr. Cantor said after racing up the stairs to get the phone. "It's boiling here. It's after seven and it's still as hot as it was at noon. The thermometers look stuck. How are you?"

"I have something to tell you. I have spectacular news," Marcia said. "Irv Schlanger got his draft notice. He's leaving camp. They need a replacement. They desperately need a waterfront director for the rest of the season. I told Mr. Blomback about you, I gave him all your credentials, and he wants to hire you, sight unseen."

Mr. Blomback was the owner-director of Indian Hill and an old friend of the Steinbergs. Before he went into the camp business, he had been a young high school vice principal in Newark and Mrs. Steinberg's boss when she was starting out as a new teacher.

"Marcia," Mr. Cantor said to her, "I've got a job."

"But you could get away from the epidemic. I'm so worried about you, Bucky. In the hot city with all those kids. In such close contact with all those kids—and right at the center of the epidemic. And that heat, day after day of that heat."

"I've got some ninety kids at the playground, and so far, among those kids we've had only four polio cases."

"Yes, and two *deaths*."

"That's still not an epidemic at the playground, Marcia."

"I meant in Weequahic altogether. It's the most affected part of the city. And it's not even August, the worst month of all. By then Weequahic could have *ten* times as many cases. Bucky, please, leave your job. You could be the boys' waterfront director at Indian Hill. The kids are great, the staff is great, Mr. Blomback is great—you'd love it here. You could be waterfront director for years and years to come. We could be working here every summer. We could be together as a couple and you'd be safe."

"I'm safe here, Marcia."

"You're *not*."

"I can't quit my job. This is my first year. How can I walk out on all those kids? I can't leave them. They need me more than ever. This is what I have to be doing."

"Darling, you're a fine and dedicated teacher, but that doesn't mean you're indispensable to a playground's summer program. *I* need you more than ever. I love you so much. I miss you so much. I dread the idea of something happening to you. What possible good are you doing our future by putting yourself in harm's way?"

"Your father deals with sick people all the time. He's in harm's way all the time. Do you worry about him that much?"

"This summer? Yes. Thank God my sisters are here at the camp. Yes, I worry about my father and about my mother and about everybody I love."

"And would you expect your father to pick up and leave his patients because of the polio?"

"My father is a doctor. He chose to be a doctor. Dealing with sick people is his job. It isn't yours. Your job is dealing with *well* people, with children who are healthy and can run around and play games and have fun. You would be a sensational waterfront director. Everybody here would love you. You're an excellent swimmer, you're an excellent diver, you're an excellent teacher. Oh, Bucky, it's a once-in-a-lifetime opportunity. And," she said, lowering her voice, "we could be alone up here. There's an island in the lake. We could canoe over there at night after lights out. We wouldn't have to worry about your grandmother or my parents or about my sisters snooping around the house. We could finally, finally be alone."

He could take all her clothes off, he thought, and see her completely naked. They could be alone on a dark island without their clothes on. And, with no one nearby to worry about, he could caress her as unhurriedly and as hungrily as he liked. And he could be free of the Kopferman family. He would not have any more Mrs. Kopfermans hysterically charging that he had given their children polio. And he could stop hating God, which was confusing his emotions and making him feel very strange. On their island he could be far from everything that was growing harder and harder to bear.

"I can't leave my grandmother," Mr. Cantor said. "How is she going to get the groceries up the three flights? She gets pains in her chest from carrying things up the stairs. I have to be here. I have to do the laundry. I have to do the shopping. I have to take care of her."

"The Einnemans can look after her for the rest of the summer. They'd go to the grocery store for her. They'd do her few pieces of laundry. They'd be more than willing to help out. She babysits for them already. They're crazy about her."

"The Einnemans are great neighbors, but it's not their job. It's mine. I can't leave Newark."

"What shall I tell Mr. Blomback?"

"Tell him thank you but I can't leave Newark, not at a time like this."

"I'm not going to tell him anything," Marcia replied. "I'm going to wait. I'm going to give you a day to think about it. I'm going to call again tomorrow night. Bucky, you most definitely wouldn't be shirking the duties of your job. There's nothing unheroic about leaving Newark at a time like this. I know you. I know what you're thinking. But you're so brave as it is, sweetheart. I get weak in the knees when I think about how brave you are. If you come to Indian Hill, you'd really just be doing another job no less conscientiously. And you'd be fulfilling another duty you have to yourself—to be happy. Bucky, this is simply prudence in the face of danger—it's common sense!"

"I'm not going to change my mind. I want to be with you, I miss you every day, but I can't possibly leave here now."

"But you must think of your own welfare too. Sleep on it, sweetheart, please, please do."

It was the Einnemans and the Fishers whom his grandmother was sitting with outside. The Fishers, an electrician and his wife in their late forties, had an eighteen-year-old son, a marine, waiting to ship out from California to the Pacific, and a daughter who was a salesgirl for the downtown department store from which his father had embezzled, an inescapable fact that would flash through Mr. Cantor's mind whenever they happened to meet leaving for work in the morning. The Einnemans were a young married couple with an infant boy who lived directly downstairs from the Cantors. The baby was outside with them, sleeping in his carriage; since the child had been born, Mr. Cantor's grandmother had been helping to look after him.

They were still talking about polio, now by recalling its frightening precursors. His grandmother was remembering when whooping cough victims were required to wear armbands and how, before a vaccine was developed, the most dreaded disease in the city was diphtheria. She remembered getting one of the first smallpox vaccinations. The site of the injection had become seriously infected, and she had a large, uneven circle of scarred flesh on her upper right arm as a result. She pushed up the half-sleeve of her housedress and extended her arm to show it to everyone.

After a while Mr. Cantor told them he was going to take a walk, and went off first to the drugstore on Avon Avenue and got an ice cream cone at the soda fountain. He chose a stool under one of the revolving fans and sat there to eat his ice cream—and to think. Any demand made upon him he had to fulfill, and the demand now was to take care of his endangered kids at the playground. And he had to fulfill it not for the kids alone but out of respect for the memory of the tenacious grocer who, with all his gruff intensity and despite all his limitations, had fulfilled every demand he ever faced. Marcia had it dead wrong—it would be hard to shun the responsibilities of his job any more execrably than by decamping to join her in the Pocono Mountains.

He could hear a siren in the distance. He heard sirens off and on, day and night now. They were not the air-raid sirens—those went off only once a week, at noon on Saturdays, and they did not induce fear so much as provide solace by proclaiming the city ready for anything. These were the sirens of ambulances going to get polio victims and transport them to the hospital, sirens stridently screaming, "Out of the way—a life is at stake!" Several city hospitals had recently run out of iron lungs, and patients in need of them were being taken to Belleville, Kearny, and Elizabeth until a new shipment of the respirator tanks reached Newark. He could only hope that the ambulance wasn't headed for the Weequahic section to pick up another of his kids.

He had begun to hear rumors that if the epidemic got any worse, all the city's playgrounds might have to be shut down in order to prevent the children from being in close contact there. Normally such a decision would be up to the Board of Health, but the mayor was opposed to any unnecessary disruption to the summer lives of Newark's boys and girls and would make the final decision himself. He was doing everything he could to calm the city's parents and, according to the paper, had appeared in each of the wards to inform concerned citizens about all the ways the city was ensuring that filth and dirt and garbage were removed regularly from public and private property. He reminded them to keep their trash cans firmly covered and to join the "Swat the Fly" campaign by keeping their screens in good repair and swatting and killing the disease-carrying flies that bred in filth and found their way indoors through open doors and unscreened windows. Garbage pickup was to be increased to every other day, and to abet the anti-fly campaign, fly swatters would be distributed free by "sanitary inspectors" visiting the residential neighborhoods to make certain that all streets were cleared of refuse. In his attempt to assure parents that everything was under control and generally safe, the mayor made a special point of telling them, "The playgrounds will remain open. Our city kids need their playgrounds in the summer. The Prudential Life Insurance Company of Newark and Metropolitan Life of New York both tell us that fresh air and sunshine are the principal weapons with which to eliminate the disease. Give the children plenty of sunshine and fresh air on the playgrounds and no germ can long withstand the impact of either. Above all," he told his audiences, "keep your yards and cellars clean, don't lose your heads, and we'll soon see a decline in the spread of this scourge. And swat the fly unmercifully. You cannot overestimate the evil that flies do."

Mr. Cantor started up Avon to Belmont swaddled by the stifling heat and enveloped by the stifling smell. On days when the wind came from the south, up from the Rahway and Linden refineries, there was the acrid smell of burning in the air, but tonight the currents were from the north, and the air had the distinctively foul stench that issued from the Secaucus pig farms, a few miles up the Hackensack River. Mr. Cantor knew of no street odor more foul. During a heat wave, when Newark seemed drained of every drop of pure air, it could sometimes be so sickeningly fecal-smelling that a strong whiff would make you gag and race indoors. People were already blaming the eruption of polio cases on the city's proximity to Secaucus—contemptuously known as "the Hog Capital of Hudson County"—and on the infectious properties inhering in that all-blanketing miasma that was, to those downwind of it, a toxic compound of God only knew what vile, pestilential, putrid ingredients. If they were right, breathing in the breath of life was a dangerous activity in Newark—take a deep breath and you could die.

Yet in spite of everything uninviting about the night, there was a string of boys on rattly old bicycles coasting full speed down the uneven cobblestones between the trolley tracks on Avon Avenue and screaming "Geronimo!" at the top of their lungs. There were boys cavorting around and grabbing at one another in front of the candy stores. There were boys seated on the tenement stoops, smoking and talking among themselves. There were boys in the middle of the street lazily tossing fly balls to one another under the streetlights. On an empty corner lot a hoop had been raised on the side wall of an abandoned building, and, by the light of the liquor store across the street, where derelicts staggered in and out, a few boys were practicing underhand foul shots. He passed another corner where some boys were gathered around a mail collection box, atop which one of their pals was perched, yodeling for their amusement. There were families camped out on fire escapes, playing radios trailing extension cords that were plugged in a wall socket inside, and more families gathered in the dim alleyways between buildings. Passing by the tenement dwellers on his walk, he saw women fanning themselves with paper fans a local dry cleaner gave free to his customers, and he saw workmen, home from the factory floor, sitting and talking in their sleeveless undershirts, and the word he heard again and again in the snatches of conversation was, of course, "polio." Only the children seemed capable of thinking of anything else. Only the children (the children!) acted as though, outside the Weequahic section at least, summertime was still a carefree adventure.

Neither on the neighborhood streets nor back at the drugstore ice cream counter did he run into any of the boys he'd grown up with and played ball with and gone through school with. By now, but for a few 4-Fs like himself—guys with heart murmurs or fallen arches or eyes as bad as his own who were working in war plants—they had all been drafted.

On Belmont, Mr. Cantor cut through the traffic at Hawthorne Avenue, where a couple of candy stores still had lights on and where he could hear the voices of boys hanging out along the street calling to one another. From there he headed up to Bergen Street and into the residential side streets of the wealthier end of the Weequahic section, on the side of the hill running down to Weequahic Park. Eventually he came to Goldsmith Avenue. Only when he was practically there did he realize that he wasn't out taking an aimless stroll halfway across the city on a hot summer night but heading very spe-

cifically for Marcia's. Maybe his intention was simply to look at the big brick house standing amid the
other large brick houses flanking it and think of her
and turn around and head back where he'd come
from. But after circling once around the block, he
found himself just paces from the Steinberg door,
and with resolve he headed up the flagstone walk
to ring the bell. The screened porch with the glider
that faced the front lawn was where Marcia and he
would sit and neck when they came back from the
movies, until her mother called from upstairs to ask
nicely if it wasn't time for Bucky to go home.

It was Dr. Steinberg who came to the door. Now
he knew why he'd been roaming far from the ten-
ements of Barclay Street, breathing in this stink-
ing air.

"Bucky, my boy," Dr. Steinberg said, opening his
arms and smiling. "What a nice surprise. Come in,
come in."

"I went to get some ice cream and took a walk
over here," Mr. Cantor explained.

"You miss your girl," Dr. Steinberg said, laughing. "So do I. I miss all three of my girls."

They went through the house to the screened
porch at the back, which looked out onto Mrs.

Steinberg's garden. Mrs. Steinberg was staying at their summer house at the shore, where, the doctor said, he would be joining her for weekends. How would Bucky like a cold drink, Dr. Steinberg asked. There was fresh lemonade in the refrigerator. He'd bring him a glass.

The Steinbergs' house was the kind Mr. Cantor had dreamed about living in when he was a kid growing up with his grandparents in their third-floor three-room flat: a large one-family house with spacious halls and a central staircase and lots of bedrooms and more than one bathroom and two screened-in porches and thick wall-to-wall carpeting in all the rooms and wooden venetian blinds covering the windows instead of Woolworth's blackout shades. And, at the rear of the house, a flower garden. He'd never seen a full-blown flower garden before, except for the renowned rose garden in Weequahic Park, which his grandmother had taken him to visit as a child. That was a public garden kept up by the parks department; as far as he'd known, *all* gardens were public. A private flower garden flourishing in a Newark backyard amazed him. His own cemented-over backyard was riven with cracks, and stretches of it were stripped of crumbling chunks that over the decades the neighborhood kids had pried loose for missiles to fling murderously at the alley cats or larkily at a passing car or in anger at one another. Girls in the building played hopscotch there until the boys drove them out to play aces up; there was the jumble of the building's beat-up metal garbage cans; and crisscrossing overhead were the clotheslines, a drooping web of them, rope strung on pulleys from a rear window in each tenement flat to a weathered telephone pole at the far side of the dilapidated yard. During earliest childhood, whenever his grandmother leaned out of the window to hang the week's wash, he stood nearby passing her the clothespins. Sometimes he would wake up screaming from nightmares of her leaning so far over the sill to hang a bedsheet that she tumbled out of the third-story window. Before his grandparents determined how and when to make intelligible to him that his mother had died in childbirth, he had come to imagine that she had died in just such a fall of her own. That's what having a backyard had meant to him until he was old enough to comprehend and deal with the truth—a place of death, a small rectangular graveyard for the women who loved him.

But now, just the thought of Mrs. Steinberg's garden filled him with pleasure and reminded him of all he valued most about the Steinbergs and how they lived, and of everything that his kindly grandparents couldn't offer him and that he'd always secretly hungered for. So unschooled was he in extravagance that he took the presence in a house of more than one bathroom as the height of luxurious living. He'd always possessed a strong family sense without himself having a traditional family, so sometimes when he was alone in the house with Marcia—which was rare because of the lively presence of her younger sisters—he would imagine that the two of them were married and the house and the garden and the domestic order and the surfeit of bathrooms were theirs. How at ease he felt in their house—yet it seemed a miracle to him that he had ever gotten there.

Dr. Steinberg came back out onto the porch with the lemonade. The porch was dark except for a lamp burning beside the chair where Dr. Steinberg had been reading the evening paper and smoking his pipe. He picked up the pipe and struck a match and, repeatedly drawing and puffing, he fussed with it until it was relit. The rich sweetness of Dr. Steinberg's tobacco served to ameliorate a little the city-wide stink of Secaucus.

Dr. Steinberg was slender, agile, on the short side. He wore a substantial mustache and glasses that, though thick, were not as thick as Mr. Cantor's. His nose was his most distinctive feature: curved like a scimitar at the top but bent flat at the tip, and with the bone of the bridge cut like a diamond—in short, a nose out of a folktale, the sort of sizable, convoluted, intricately turned nose that, for many centuries, confronted though they have been by every imaginable hardship, the Jews had never stopped making. The irregularity of the nose was most conspicuous when he laughed, which he did often. He was unfailingly friendly, one of those engaging family physicians who, when they step into the waiting room holding someone's file folder, make the faces of all their patients light up—whenever he came at them with his stethoscope, they'd find themselves acutely happy to be under his care. Marcia liked that her father, a man of natural, unadorned authority, would jokingly but truthfully refer to his patients as his "masters."

"Marcia told me that you've lost some of your

boys. I'm sorry to hear that, Bucky. Death is not that common among polio victims."

"So far, four have gotten polio and two have died. Two boys. Grade school boys. Both twelve."

"It's a lot of responsibility for you," Dr. Steinberg said, "looking after all those boys, especially at a time like this. I've been practicing medicine for over twenty-five years, and when I lose a patient, even if it's to old age, I still feel shaken. This epidemic must be a great weight on your shoulders."

"The problem is, I don't know if I'm doing the right thing or not by letting them play ball."

"Did anyone say you're doing the wrong thing?"

"Yes, the mother of two of the boys, brothers, who have gotten polio. I know she was hysterical. I know she was lashing out in frustration, yet knowing it doesn't seem to help."

"A doctor runs into that too. You're right—people in great pain become hysterical and, confronted with the injustice of illness, they lash out. But boys' playing ball doesn't give them polio. A virus does. We may not know much about polio, but we know that. Kids everywhere play hard out of doors all summer long, and even in an epidemic it's a very small percentage who become infected with the disease. And a very small percentage of those who get seriously ill from it. And a very small percentage of those who die—death results from respiratory paralysis, which is relatively rare. Every child who gets a headache doesn't come down with paralytic polio. That's why it's important not to exaggerate the danger and to carry on normally. You have nothing to feel guilty about. That's a natural reaction sometimes, but in your case it's not justified." Pointing at him meaningfully with the stem of his pipe, he warned the young man, "We can be severe judges of ourselves when it is in no way warranted. A misplaced sense of responsibility can be a debilitating thing."

"Dr. Steinberg, do you think it's going to get worse?"

"Epidemics have a way of spontaneously running out of steam. Right now there's a lot going on. Right now we have to keep up with what's happening while we wait and see whether this is fleeting or not. Usually the great majority of the cases are children under five. That's how it was in 1916. The pattern we're seeing with this outbreak, at least here in Newark, is somewhat different. But that doesn't suggest that the disease is going to go unchecked in this city forever. There's still no cause for alarm as far as I can tell."

Mr. Cantor hadn't felt as relieved in weeks as he did while being counseled by Dr. Steinberg. There was no place in all of Newark, including his family's flat—including even the gym floor at Chancellor Avenue School where he taught his phys ed classes—where he felt any more content than he did on the screened-in porch at the rear of the Steinberg home, with Dr. Steinberg seated in his cushioned wicker armchair and pulling on his well-worn pipe.

"Why is the epidemic worst in the Weequahic section?" Mr. Cantor asked. "Why should that be?"

"I don't know," Dr. Steinberg said. "Nobody knows. Polio is still a mysterious disease. It was slow coming this time. At first it was mainly in the Ironbound, then it jumped around the city, and suddenly it settled in Weequahic and took off."

Mr. Cantor told Dr. Steinberg about the incident with the East Side High Italians who'd driven up from the Ironbound and left the pavement at the playground entrance awash with their spit.

"You did the right thing," Dr. Steinberg told him. "You cleaned it up with water and ammonia. That was the best thing to do."

"But did I kill the polio germs, if there were any?"

"We don't know what kills polio germs," Dr. Steinberg said. "We don't know who or what carries polio, and there's still some debate about how it enters the body. But what's important is that you cleaned up an unhygienic mess and reassured the boys by the way you took charge. You demonstrated your competence, you demonstrated your equanimity—that's what the kids have to see. Bucky, you're shaken by what's happening now, but strong men get the shakes too. You must understand that a lot of us who are much older and more experienced with illness than you are also shaken by it. To stand by as a doctor unable to stop the spread of this dreadful disease is painful for all of us. A crippling disease that attacks mainly children and leaves some of them dead—that's difficult for any adult to accept. You have a conscience, and a conscience is a valuable attribute, but not if it begins to make you think you're to blame for what is far beyond the scope of your responsibility."

He thought to ask: Doesn't God have a conscience? Where's His responsibility? Or does He
know no limits? But instead he asked, "Should the
playground be shut down?"

"You're the director. Should it?" Dr. Steinberg
asked.

"I don't know what to think."

"What would the boys do if they couldn't come
to the playground? Stay at home? No, they'd play
ball somewhere else—in the streets, in the empty
lots, they'd go down to the park to play ball. You
can't get them to stop congregating together just by
expelling them from the playground. They won't
stay home—they'll hang around the corner candy
store together, banging the pinball machine and
pushing and shoving one another for fun. They'll
drink out of each other's soda bottles no matter how
much you tell them not to. Some of them will be
so restless and bored they'll go too far and get into
trouble. They're not angels—they're boys. Bucky,
there's nothing you're doing that's making things
worse. To the contrary, you're making things better.
You're doing something useful. You're contributing
to the welfare of the community. It's important that
neighborhood life goes on as usual—otherwise, it's

not only the stricken and their families who are victims, but Weequahic itself becomes a victim. At the playground you help keep panic at bay by overseeing those kids of yours playing the games they love. The alternative isn't to send them someplace else where they won't have your supervision. The alternative isn't to lock them up in their houses and fill them with dread. I'm against the frightening of Jewish kids. I'm against the frightening of Jews, period. That was Europe, that's why Jews fled. This is America. The less fear the better. Fear unmans us. Fear degrades us. Fostering less fear—that's your job and mine."

There were sirens in the distance, off to the west where the hospital was. In the garden there were only shrill crickets and pulsating lightning bugs and the many varieties of fragrant flowers, their petals massed on the other side of the porch screens and, with Mrs. Steinberg away at the shore, more than likely watered by Dr. Steinberg after he'd eaten his dinner. A bowl of fruit lay on the glass top of the wicker coffee table in front of the wicker sofa where Mr. Cantor was sitting. Dr. Steinberg reached for a piece of fruit and told Mr. Cantor to help himself.

He bit into a delicious peach, a big and beauti-

ful peach like the one Dr. Steinberg had taken from
the bowl, and in the company of this thoroughly
reasonable man and the soothing sense of security
he exuded, he took his time eating it, savoring every
sweet mouthful right down to the pit. Then, wholly
unprepared for the moment but unable to contain
himself, he placed the pit into an ashtray, leaned
forward, and compressing his sticky hands tightly
together between his knees, he said, "I would like
your permission, sir, to ask Marcia to become engaged."

Dr. Steinberg burst out laughing and, raising his
pipe in the air as though it were a trophy, he stood
and did a little jig. "You have it!" he said. "I couldn't
be more thrilled. And Mrs. Steinberg will be just as
thrilled. I'm going to call her right now. And you're
going to get on and tell her the news yourself. Oh,
Bucky, this is just swell! Of course you have our
permission. Marcia couldn't have hooked herself a
better fellow. What a lucky family we are!"

Startled to hear Dr. Steinberg characterize *his*
family as the lucky ones, Mr. Cantor felt himself
flush with excitement, and he jumped to his feet too
and heartily shook Dr. Steinberg's hand. Until that
moment he hadn't planned to mention engagement

to anyone until the new year, when he would be a
bit more secure financially. He was still saving to
buy a gas stove for his grandmother, to replace the
coal stove she cooked on in the kitchen, and had
figured that he'd have enough by December, if he
didn't have to buy an engagement ring before then.
But it was all the comfort he had derived from her
kindly father, concluding with their enjoying those
perfect peaches together on the back porch, that
had roused him to seek permission there and then.
What had done it was his knowing that Dr. Steinberg, merely by his presence, seemed able to answer the questions that nobody else could: what the
hell is going on, and how do we get out of this?
And something else had galvanized him as well: the
sound of the ambulance sirens crisscrossing Newark in the night.

THE NEXT MORNING was the worst so far. Three
more boys had come down with polio—Leo Feinswog, Paul Lippman, and me, Arnie Mesnikoff.
The playground had jumped from four to seven
cases overnight. The sirens that he and Dr. Steinberg had heard the evening before could well have

been from the ambulances speeding them to the
hospital. He learned about the three new cases from
the kids who came with their mitts that morning
ready to spend the day playing ball. On an ordinary
weekday he'd have two games going, one at each of
the diamonds at either corner of the playground,
but on this morning there weren't nearly enough
boys on hand to field four teams. Aside from those
who had taken ill, some sixty had apparently been
kept away by apprehensive parents. The remainder
he gathered together to talk to on the section of
wooden bleachers that backed on to the rear wall
of the school.

"Boys, I'm glad to see you here. Today's going
to be another scorcher—you can tell that already.
But that doesn't mean we're not going to go out
on the field and play. It does mean we're going to
take some precautions so none of you overdo it.
Every two and a half innings we're taking a break
in the shade, right here on the bleachers, for fifteen minutes. No running around during that time.
That means everybody. Between noon and two,
when it's hottest, there's going to be no softball at
all. The ball fields are going to be empty. You want

to play checkers, chess, Ping-Pong, you want to sit and talk on the bleachers, you want to bring a book or a magazine with you to read during the time-out . . . that's all fine. That's our new daily schedule. We're going to have as good a summer as we can, but we're going to do everything in moderation on days like this. Nobody here is going to get sunstroke out in that savage heat." He inserted "sunstroke" at the last moment, instead of saying "polio."

There were no complaints. There were no comments at all. They listened solemnly and nodded in agreement. It was the first time since the epidemic had begun that he could sense their fear. They each knew more than casually one or another of those who'd come down with the disease the day before, and in a way that they hadn't previously grasped the nature of the threat, they at last understood the chance they stood of catching polio themselves.

Mr. Cantor picked two teams of ten to start the first game. There were ten kids left over, and he told them they would go on to substitute, five to a side, after the first fifteen-minute break. That's the way they'd proceed throughout the day.

"All right?" Mr. Cantor said, clapping his hands

enthusiastically. "It's a summer day like any other, and I want you to go out and play ball."

Instead of playing himself, he decided to start off the morning by sitting with the ten boys who were waiting their turn to join the game and who seemed unusually subdued. Back of center field, where the girls regularly gathered in the school street, Mr. Cantor noted that of the original dozen or so who had begun meeting there every weekday morning earlier in the summer, only three were present today—only three whose parents would apparently allow them to leave the vicinity of their homes for fear of their making contact with the other playground kids. The missing girls may have been among the neighborhood children he'd heard about who had been sent to take refuge with relatives a safe distance from the city, and some among those whisked from the menace to be immersed in, immunized by, the hygienic ocean air of the Jersey Shore.

Now two of the girls were turning the rope while one was jumping—and with nobody any longer quivering on her skinny legs, ready to rush in after her. The jumper's high tweeting voice could be heard that morning as far away as the bleachers, where boys normally full of jokes and wisecracks who had no trouble blabbering away all day long found themselves now with nothing to say.

> K, my name is Kay
> And my husband's name is Karl,
> We come from Kansas
> And we bring back kangaroos!

Mr. Cantor finally broke the long silence. "Any of you have friends who got sick?" he asked them.

They either nodded or quietly said yes.

"That's tough for you, I know. Very tough. We have to hope they get better and that they're soon back on the playground."

"You can wind up in an iron lung forever," said Bobby Finkelstein, a shy boy who was among the quietest of them, one of the boys he'd seen wearing a suit on the steps of the synagogue after Alan Michaels's funeral service.

"You can," said Mr. Cantor. "But that's from respiratory paralysis, and that's very rare. You're far more likely to recover. It's a serious disease, it can do great harm, but there are recoveries. Sometimes they're partial, but many times they're total. Most cases are relatively light." He spoke with authority, the source of his knowledge being Dr. Steinberg.

"You can die," Bobby said, pursuing this subject in a way that in the past he'd pursued few others. Mostly he seemed to enjoy letting the extroverts do the talking, yet about what had happened to his friends he could not keep himself from going on. "Alan and Herbie died."

"You can die," Mr. Cantor allowed, "but the chances are slight."

"They weren't slight for Alan and Herbie," Bobby replied.

"I meant the chances are slight overall in the community, in the city."

"That doesn't help Alan and Herbie," Bobby insisted, his voice quavering.

"You're right, Bobby. You're right. It doesn't. What happened to them was terrible. What's happened to all the boys is terrible."

Now another of the boys on the bleachers spoke up, Kenny Blumenfeld, though what he was saying was unintelligible because of the state he was in. He was a tall, strong boy, intelligent, articulate, already at fourteen in his second year at Weequahic High and, unlike most of the other boys, mature in his ability to put emotion aside in matters of winning and losing. He, along with Alan, had been a leader on the playground, the boy who was always chosen captain of a team, the boy who had the longest arms and legs and hit the longest ball—and yet it was Kenny, the oldest and biggest and most grown-up of them all, as sturdy emotionally as he was physically, who was drumming his clenched fists on his thighs as tears coursed down his face.

Mr. Cantor went over to where he was seated and sat next to him.

Through his tears, speaking hoarsely, Kenny said, "All my friends are getting polio! All my friends are going to be cripples or going to be dead!"

In response Mr. Cantor placed his hand on Kenny's shoulder but said nothing. He looked out onto the field where the two teams were deep in the game, oblivious of what was happening on the sidelines. He remembered Dr. Steinberg cautioning him not to exaggerate the danger, and yet he thought: Kenny's right. Every one of them. Those on the field and those on the bleachers. The girls jumping rope. They're all kids, and polio is going after kids, and it will sweep through this place and destroy them all. Each morning that I show up there'll be another few gone. There's nothing to stop it unless they shut down the playground. And even shutting it down won't help—in the end it's going to get every last child. The neighborhood is doomed. Not a one of the children will survive intact, if they survive at all.

And then, out of nowhere, he thought of that peach he'd eaten on the Steinbergs' back porch the night before. He could all but feel its juice trickling onto his hand, and for the first time he was frightened for himself. What was amazing was how long he had kept the fear in check.

He watched Kenny Blumenfeld weeping over his friends beset by polio, and suddenly he wanted to flee from working in the midst of these kids—to flee from the unceasing awareness of the persistent peril. To flee, as Marcia wanted him to.

Instead he sat quietly beside Kenny until the crying had subsided. Then he told him, "I'll be back— I'm going to play for a while." He stepped down off the bleachers and walked onto the field, where he said to Barry Mittelman, the third baseman, "Get out of the sun now, get in the shade, get some water," and taking Barry's mitt, he installed himself at third, vigorously working the pocket with his knuckles.

By the end of the day, Mr. Cantor had played at every position on the field, giving the boys on either side a chance to sit out an inning in the shade so as not to get overheated. He did not know what else to do to prevent the polio from spreading. Playing in the outfield, he'd had to hold his glove up to the peak of his baseball cap in order not to be blinded by the sun, a four o'clock sun no less punishing than the twelve o'clock sledgehammer. To his surprise, just beyond him on the school street he could hear the three sun-baked girls, still feverishly at it, still thrilling to the cadences of a thumping heart.

> S, my name is Sally
> And my husband's name is Sam . . .

At about five, when the boys were into the final inning of the last game of the day—the fielders with their sopping polo shirts cast aside on the nearby asphalt and the boys in the batter's box shirtless too— Mr. Cantor heard loud hollering from deep center field. It was Kenny Blumenfeld, enraged with, of all people, Horace. Mr. Cantor had noticed Horace down at the end of the bench earlier in the afternoon but soon lost track of him and couldn't remember seeing him again. Probably he'd gone off to meander around the neighborhood and had only just returned to the playground and, disposed as he was to go out onto the field and stand silent and motionless beside one of the players, had chosen to approach Kenny and be near the biggest boy on either team. Earlier in the day it was Kenny who, uncharacteristically, had been racked with sobs about the ravaging of his friends, and now, again uncharacteristically, it was Kenny who was shouting at Horace and threateningly waving him off with his mitt. Not only was Kenny the biggest boy, but without his shirt on it was apparent that he was the strongest one too. By contrast, Horace, wearing his usual summer outfit of an oversized half-sleeve shirt and ballooning cotton trousers with an elasticized waistband and long-outmoded brown-and-white perforated shoes, seemed undernourished to the point of emaciation. His chest was sunken, his legs were spindly, and his scrawny marionette arms, dangling weakly at his sides, looked as if you could snap them in two as easily as you break a stick over your knee. He looked as though a good fright could kill him, let alone a blow from a boy built like Kenny.

Instantly, Mr. Cantor sprang off the bench where he was seated and ran at full speed to the outfield while all the boys in the game and on the bleachers ran along with him and the three girls on the street stopped jumping rope, seemingly for the first time all summer.

"Get him away from me!" Kenny—the boy who was the model of maturity for the others, whom Mr. Cantor never had reason to admonish for failing to exercise self-control—that same Kenny was now howling, "Get him away from me or I'll kill him!"

"What is it? What's going on?" Mr. Cantor asked. Horace stood there with his head hanging and tears rolling down his face and keening, emitting a kind of radio signal from high in the back of his throat—a thin, oscillating sound of distress.

"Smell him!" Kenny screamed. "He has shit all over him! Get him the hell away from me! It's him! He's the one who's carrying the polio!"

"Calm down, Ken," Mr. Cantor said, trying to take hold of the boy, who wildly fought his way free. They were surrounded by the players on both teams now, and when several of the boys rushed forward to grab Kenny by the arms and pull him back from where he was excoriating Horace, he turned to strike out at them with his fists, and all of them jumped away.

"I'm not calming down!" Kenny cried. "He's got shit all over his underwear! He's got shit all over his hands! He doesn't wash and he isn't clean, and then he wants us to take his hand, and shake his hand, and that's how he's spreading polio! He's the one who's crippling people! He's the one who's killing people! Get out of here, you! Get! Go!" And again he waved his mitt violently in the air as though warding off the attack of a rabid dog.

Meanwhile, managing to keep clear of Kenny's flailing arms, Mr. Cantor was able to interpose himself between the hysterical boy and the terrified creature onto whom he was pouring out his rage.

"You have to go home, Horace," Mr. Cantor quietly told him. "Go home to your parents. It's time for your supper. It's time to eat."

Horace did smell—he smelled horribly. And though Mr. Cantor repeated his words a second time, Horace kept on crying and keening and saying nothing.

"Here, Horace," Mr. Cantor said and extended his hand to him. Without looking up, Horace took the hand limply in his and Mr. Cantor shook Horace's hand as heartily as he had shaken Dr. Steinberg's after receiving his permission to become engaged to Marcia the night before.

"How ya doin', Horace?" Mr. Cantor whispered, pumping Horace's hand up and down. "How ya doin', boy?" It took a little longer than usual, but then, just as it always had in the past when Horace moseyed out to stand beside a player on the field, the handshake ritual did the trick, and Horace, assuaged, turned toward the playground exit to leave, whether for home or elsewhere nobody knew, probably not even Horace. All the boys who had heard Kenny's raving hung way back from Horace as they watched him lurch off alone into the wall of heat, while the girls, shrilly screaming "He's after us! The moron is chasing us!" ran with their jump ropes toward the late-afternoon Chancellor Avenue traffic, ran as fast as they could from the sight of how deep the human blight can go.

To quiet Kenny down, Mr. Cantor asked him to stay behind when the rest of the boys headed off and to help him put the playground equipment away in the basement storage room. Then, quietly talking to Kenny as they walked, Mr. Cantor accompanied him to his house, down the hill on Hansbury Avenue.

"It's piling up on everyone, Ken. You're not the only one in the neighborhood," he told him, "who's feeling the pressure of the polio. Between the polio and the weather, there isn't anybody who isn't at the end of his rope."

"But he's spreading it, Mr. Cantor. I'm sure of it. I shouldn't have gone nuts, I know he's a moron, but he's not clean and he's spreading it. He walks all over the place and drools over everything and shakes everyone's hand and that's how he spreads the germs everywhere."

"First off, Ken, we don't know what spreads it."

"But we *do*. Filth, dirt, and shit," Kenny said, his outrage revving up again. "And he's filthy, dirty, and shitty, and he's spreading it. I know it."

On the pavement in front of Kenny's house, Mr. Cantor took him firmly by his shoulders, and Kenny, shuddering with revulsion, instantly shook free of his hands and cried, "Don't touch me! You just touched him!"

"Go inside," Mr. Cantor said, still composed but

retreating a step. "Take a cold shower. Get a cold drink. Cool off, Ken, and I'll see you tomorrow up at the playground."

"But you're only being blind to who's spreading it because he's so helpless! Only he's not just helpless—he's dangerous! Don't you understand, Mr. Cantor? He doesn't know how to wipe his ass, so he gets it all over everyone else!"

THAT EVENING, watching his grandmother while she served him his dinner, he found himself wondering if this was how his mother would have come to look if she had been lucky enough to live another fifty years—frail, stooped, brittle-boned, with hair that decades earlier had lost its darkness and thinned to a white fluff, with stringy skin in the crooks of her arms and a fleshy lobe hanging from her chin and joints that ached in the morning and ankles that swelled and throbbed by nightfall and translucent papery skin on her mottled hands and cataracts that had shrouded and discolored her vision. As for the face above the ruin of her neck, it was now a tightly drawn mesh of finely patterned wrinkles, grooves so minute they appeared to be the work of an implement far less crude than the truncheon of old age—an etching needle perhaps, or a lacemaker's tool, manipulated by a master craftsman to render her as ancient-looking a grandmother as any on earth.

There had been a strong resemblance between his mother and his grandmother when his mother was growing up. He had seen it in photographs, where, of course, he had first noticed his own strong resemblance to his mother, particularly in the framed studio portrait of her that rested on the bureau in his grandparents' bedroom. The picture, taken for her high school graduation when she was eighteen, was in the 1919 South Side yearbook that Bucky leafed through often as a young schoolboy beginning to discover that the other boys in his class were not grandsons living with grandparents but sons living with a mother and father in what he came to think of as "real families." He best understood how precarious his footing in the world was when adults bestowed upon him the look that he despised, the pitying look that he knew so well, since he sometimes got it from teachers too. The look made only too clear that the intervention of his mother's aging parents was all that had stood between him and the bleak four-story red-brick building on nearby Clinton Avenue with its black iron fence and its windows of pebbled glass covered with iron grates and its heavy wooden doorway adorned with a white Jewish star and the broad lintel above it carved with the three most forlorn words he'd ever read: HEBREW ORPHAN ASYLUM.

Even though the graduation picture on the bedroom bureau was said by his grandmother to catch perfectly the kindly spirit that animated his mother, it was not his favorite photograph of her, because of the dark academic robe she wore over her dress, the sight of which never failed to sadden him, as if the robe in the picture were a portent, the harbinger of her shroud. Nonetheless, alone at home when his grandparents were working around the corner in the store, he would sometimes drift into his grandparents' room to run the tip of one finger over the glass that protected the picture, tracing the contours of his mother's face as though the glass had been removed and the face there was flesh. He did this despite its causing him to feel keenly not the presence he was seeking but rather the absence of one he'd never seen anywhere other than in photos, whose voice he'd never heard speaking his name, whose maternal warmth he'd never luxuriated in, a

mother who had never got to care for him or feed
him or put him to bed or help him with his schoolwork or watch him grow up to be the first of the
family slated to go to college. Yet could he truthfully say he hadn't been sufficiently cherished as a
child? Why was the genuine tenderness of a loving
grandmother any less satisfying than the tenderness
of a mother? It shouldn't have been, and yet secretly he felt that it was—and secretly felt ashamed
for harboring such a thought.

After all this time, it had suddenly occurred to
Mr. Cantor that God wasn't simply letting polio
rampage through the Weequahic section but that
twenty-three years back, God had also allowed
his mother, only two years out of high school and
younger than he was now, to die in childbirth. He'd
never thought about her death that way before. Previously, because of the loving care that he received
from his grandparents, it had always seemed to him
that losing his mother at birth was something that
was meant to happen to him and that his grandparents' raising him was a natural consequence of her
death. So too was his father's being a gambler and a
thief something that was meant to happen and that
couldn't have been otherwise. But now that he was

no longer a child he was capable of understanding that why things couldn't be otherwise was because of God. If not for God, if not for the *nature* of God, they *would* be otherwise.

He couldn't repeat such an idea to his grandmother, who was no more reflective than his grandfather had been, and he did not feel inclined to talk about it with Dr. Steinberg. Though very much a thinking man, Dr. Steinberg was also an observant Jew and might take offense at the turn of mind that the polio epidemic was inspiring in Mr. Cantor. He wouldn't want to affront any of the Steinbergs, least of all Marcia, for whom the High Holidays were a source of reverence and a time of prayer when she dutifully attended synagogue services with her family on all three days. He wanted to show respect for everything that the Steinbergs held dear, including, of course, the religion that he shared with them, even if, like his grandfather—for whom duty was a religion, rather than the other way around—he was an indifferent practitioner of it. And to be wholly respectful had always been easy enough until the moment he found his anger provoked because of all the kids he was losing to polio, including the incorrigible Kopferman boys. His anger provoked not against the Italians or the houseflies or the mail or the milk or the money or malodorous Secaucus or the merciless heat or Horace, not against whatever cause, however unlikely, people, in their fear and confusion, might advance to explain the epidemic, not even against the polio virus, but against the source, the creator—against God, who made the virus.

"YOU'RE NOT WEARING yourself down, are you, Eugene?" Dinner was over and he was cleaning up while she sat at the table sipping a glass of water from the icebox. "You rush to the playground," she said, "you rush to visit the families of your boys, you rush on Sunday to the funeral, you rush home in the evening to help me—maybe this weekend you should stop rushing around in this heat and take the train and find a bed for the weekend down the shore. Take a break from everything. Get away from the heat. Get away from the playground. Go swimming. It'll do you a world of good."

"That's a thought, Grandma. That's not a bad idea."

"The Einnemans can look in on me, and Sunday night you'll come home refreshed. This polio is wearing you out. That's no good for anyone."

Over dinner he had told her about the three new cases at the playground and said that he was going to telephone the families later, when they got home from the hospital.

Meanwhile, the sirens were sounding again, and very close to the house, which was unusual, since as far as he knew there'd been no more than three or four cases in the entire residential triangle formed by Springfield, Clinton, and Belmont avenues. Theirs were the lowest numbers for any neighborhood in the city. At the southern end of the triangle, where he lived with his grandmother and where the rents were half what they were in Weequahic, there had been but a single case of polio—the victim an adult, a man of thirty, a stevedore who worked at the port—while in the Weequahic section, with its five elementary schools, there had been more than a hundred and forty cases, all in children under fourteen, in the first weeks of July alone.

Yes, of course—the shore, where some of his playground kids had already escaped with their mothers for the remainder of the summer. He knew a rooming house back from the beach in Bradley where he could get one of the cots in the cellar for a buck. He could do his diving off the high board of the boardwalk's big saltwater pool, dive all day long and then at night stroll along the boards to Asbury Park and pick up a mess of fried clams and a root beer at the arcade and sit on one of the benches facing the ocean and happily feast away while watching the surf come crashing in. What could be more removed from the Newark polio epidemic, what could be more of a tonic for him, than the booming black nighttime Atlantic? This was the first summer since the war began when the danger of German U-boats in nearby waters or of waterborne German saboteurs coming ashore after dark was considered to be over, when the blackout had been lifted, and—though the coast guard still patrolled the beaches and maintained pillboxes along the coast—when the lights were on again all along the Jersey Shore. That meant that both the Germans and the Japanese were suffering crippling defeats and that, nearly three years after it had begun, America's war was beginning to come to an end. It meant that his two best college buddies, Big Jake Garonzik and Dave Jacobs, would be returning home unscathed, if only they could make it through the remaining months of combat in Europe. He thought of the song Marcia liked so much: "I'll be seeing you in all the old familiar places." That will be the day, he thought, when he could see Jake and Dave in the old familiar places!

He had never gotten over the shame of not being with them, for all that there was nothing he could do about it. They had wound up together in an airborne unit, jumping from planes into battle—what he would have wanted to do, exactly what he was *constructed* to do. Some six weeks earlier, at dawn on D-Day, they had been members of a huge paratroop force that had landed behind the German lines on the Normandy peninsula. Mr. Cantor knew from staying in touch with their families that despite the many casualties taken during the invasion, the two of them had survived. From following the maps in the paper plotting the Allies' progress, he figured that they had probably been in the heavy fighting to capture Cherbourg late in June. The first thing Mr. Cantor looked for in the *Newark News* that his grandmother got from the Einnemans every night after they'd finished reading it was whatever he could find about the U.S.

army's campaign in France. After that, he read the box on the front page of the *News* that was called "The Daily Polio Bulletin" and that appeared just below a reproduction of a quarantine sign. "Board of Health of Newark, New Jersey," the sign read. "Keep out. This house contains a case of polio. Any person violating the isolation and quarantine rules and regulations of the board or who willfully removes, defaces, or obstructs this card without authority is liable to a fine of $50." The polio bulletin, which was also broadcast every day on the local radio station, kept Newarkers up to date on the number and location of every new case in the city. So far this summer, what people heard or read there was never what they hoped to find there—that the epidemic was on the wane—but rather that the tally of new cases had increased yet again from the day before. The impact of the numbers was, of course, disheartening and frightening and wearying. For these weren't the impersonal numbers one was accustomed to hearing on the radio or reading in the paper, the numbers that served to locate a house or record a person's age or establish the price of a pair of shoes. These were the terrifying numbers charting the progress of a horrible disease and, in the sixteen wards of Newark, corresponding in their impact to the numbers of the dead, wounded, and missing in the real war. Because this was real war too, a war of slaughter, ruin, waste, and damnation, war with the ravages of war—war upon the children of Newark.

YES, HE COULD certainly use a few days on his own down the shore. That, in fact, was what he'd been planning on doing when the summer began—with Marcia gone, to head to the shore every weekend to dive the day away and then walk the boards to Asbury at night to eat his favorite seashore meal. The cellar was dank where he rented a cot and the water was rarely hot in the shower everyone used and there was sand in the sheets and towels, but, second only to throwing the javelin, diving was his favorite sport. Two days of diving would help him to shake loose, at least temporarily, from the preoccupation with his stricken boys and quiet his agitation over Kenny Blumenfeld's hysterical outbursts and maybe clear his head of the malice he felt toward God.

Then, when his grandmother was outside with the neighbors and he was about finished with cleaning up and had just sat down at the table in his sleeveless undershirt and briefs to drink yet another glass of ice water, Marcia called. Dr. Steinberg had agreed to wait for Mr. Cantor to talk with Marcia before he or Mrs. Steinberg said anything to her about the engagement, so she was calling without any knowledge of the conversation on the back porch the evening before. She was calling to tell him she loved him and she missed him and to learn what he had decided about coming to the camp to take over from Irv Schlanger as waterfront director.

"What should I tell Mr. Blomback?" she asked.

"Tell him yes," Mr. Cantor said, and he startled himself no less by what he'd just agreed to than he had done asking permission of Dr. Steinberg to become engaged to his daughter. "Tell him I will," he said.

Yet he'd had every intention of taking his grandmother's suggestion and going to the shore for the weekend and marshaling his forces so as to return to his job rejuvenated. If Jake and Dave could parachute into Nazi-occupied France on D-Day and help to anchor the Allied beachhead by fighting their way into Cherbourg against the stiffest German opposition, then surely he could face the dangers of running the playground at Chancellor Avenue School in the midst of a polio epidemic.

"Oh, Bucky," cried Marcia, "that's swell! Knowing you, I was so frightened you were going to say no. Oh, you're coming, you're coming to Indian Hill!"

"I'll have to call O'Gara and tell him, and he'll have to get somebody to take my place. O'Gara's the guy in charge of playgrounds at the superintendent's office. That could take a couple of days."

"Oh, do it as fast as you can!"

"I'll have to speak to Mr. Blomback myself. About the salary. I've got the rent and my grandmother to think about."

"I'm sure the salary's going to be no problem."

"And I have to talk to you about getting engaged," he said.

"What? You what?"

"We're getting engaged, Marcia. That's why I'm taking the job. I asked your father's permission last night over at the house. I'm coming to camp and we're getting engaged."

"We are?" she said, laughing. "Isn't it customary for the girl to be asked, even a girl as pliant as me?"

"Is it? I've never done it before. Will you be my fiancée?"

"Of course! Oh my goodness, Bucky, I'm so happy!"

"So am I," he said, "tremendously happy," and for the moment, because of this happiness, he was almost able to forget the betrayal of his playground kids; he was almost able to forget his outrage with God for the murderous persecution of Weequahic's innocent children. Talking to Marcia about their engagement, he was almost able to look the other way and to rush to embrace the security and predictability and contentment of a normal life lived in normal times. But when he hung up, there confronting him were his ideals—ideals of truthfulness and strength fostered in him by his grandfather, ideals of courage and sacrifice that he shared with Jake and Dave, ideals nurtured by him in boyhood to place himself beyond the reach of a crooked father's penchant for deceit—his ideals as a man demanding of him that he immediately reverse course and return for the rest of the summer to the work he had contracted to perform.

How could he have done what he'd just done?

*

IN THE MORNING he carried the equipment up from the storage room and organized two teams and got a softball game under way for the fewer than twenty kids who'd shown up to play. Then he returned to the basement to call O'Gara from his office and tell him that he was leaving his job at the end of the week to take over as waterfront director at a summer camp in the Poconos. That morning before he'd left for the playground, he'd gotten news over the radio that there were twenty-nine new polio cases in the city, sixteen of them in Weequahic.

"That's the second guy this morning," O'Gara said. "I got a Jewish guy over at Peshine Avenue playground who's quitting on me too." O'Gara was a tired old man with a big gut and an antagonistic manner who'd been running the city playgrounds for years and whose prowess as a Central High football player at the time of the First World War still constituted the culmination of his life. His brusqueness wasn't necessarily killing, yet it unsettled Mr. Cantor and left him feeling shifty and childishly grubbing about for the words to justify his decision. O'Gara's brusqueness wasn't unlike his grandfather's, perhaps because it was acquired on the

same tough streets of the Third Ward. His grandfather was, of course, the last person he wanted to
be thinking about while doing something so out of
keeping with who he really was. He wanted to be
thinking about Marcia and the Steinbergs and the
future, but instead there was his grandfather to deliver the verdict with just a bit of an Irish intona-
tion.

"The fellow I'm taking over for at the camp has
been drafted," Mr. Cantor responded. "I've got to
leave on Friday for the camp."

"This is what I get for giving you a plum job just
a year out of college. You realize that you haven't
exactly won my confidence by pulling a stunt like
this. You realize that leaving me in the lurch in July
like this isn't likely to make me disposed to ever
hire you again, Cancer."

"Cantor," Mr. Cantor corrected him, as he always had to when they spoke.

"I don't care how many guys are away in the
army," O'Gara said. "I don't like people quitting on
me right in the midst of everything." And then he
added, "Especially people who *aren't* in the army."

"I'm sorry to be leaving, Mr. O'Gara. And," he
said, speaking in a shriller tone than he'd intended,

"I'm sorry I'm not in the army—sorrier than you know." To make matters worse, he added, "I have to go. I have no choice."

"What?" O'Gara snapped back. "You have no choice, do you? Sure you got a choice. What you're doing is called making a choice. You're making your escape from the polio. You sign up for a job, and then there's the polio, and the hell with the job, the hell with the commitment, you run like hell as fast as you can. All you're doing is running away, Cancer, a world-champion muscleman like you. You're an opportunist, Cancer. I could say worse, but that will do." And then, with revulsion, he repeated, "An opportunist," as though the word stood for every degrading instinct that could possibly stigmatize a man.

"I have a fiancée at the camp," Mr. Cantor replied lamely.

"You had a fiancée at the camp when you signed on at Chancellor."

"No, no, I didn't," he rushed to say, as if to O'Gara that would make a difference. "We only became engaged this week."

"All right, you got an answer for everything. Like the guy from Peshine. You Jewish boys got all the answers. No, you're not stupid—*but neither is O'Gara, Cancer.* All right, all right, I'll get somebody up there to take your place, if there is anyone in this town who can fill your shoes. In the meantime, you have a rollicking time roasting marshmallows with your girlfriend at your kiddie camp."

It was no less humiliating than he'd thought it would be, but he'd done it and it was over. He just had to get through three more days at the playground without contracting polio.

2

Indian Hill

He'd never been to the Pocono Mountains before, or up through the rural northwestern counties of New Jersey to Pennsylvania. The train ride, traversing hills and woods and open farmland, made him think of himself as on a far greater excursion than just traveling to the next state over. There was an epic dimension to gliding past a landscape wholly unfamiliar to him, a sense he'd had the few previous times he'd been aboard a train—including the Jersey line that carried him to the shore—that a future new and unknown to him was about to unfold. Sighting the Delaware Water Gap, where the river separating New Jersey and Pennsylvania cut dramatically through the mountain range just fifteen minutes from his stop at Stroudsburg, only heightened the intensity of the trip and assured him—

admittedly without reason—that no destroyer could possibly overleap so grand a natural barrier in order to catch him.

This marked the first time since his grandfather's death, three years earlier, that he would be leaving his grandmother in the care of anyone else for more than a weekend, and the first time he'd be out of the city for more than a night or two. And it was the first time in weeks that thoughts of polio weren't swamping him. He still mourned the two boys who had died, he was still oppressed by thinking of all of his other boys stricken with the crippling disease, yet he did not feel that he had faltered under the exigencies of the calamity or that someone else could have performed his job any more zealously. With all his energy and ingenuity, he had wholeheartedly confronted a devastating challenge—until he had chosen to abandon the challenge and flee the torrid city trembling under its epidemic and resounding with the sirens of ambulances constantly on the move.

At the Stroudsburg station, Carl, the Indian Hill driver, a large baby-faced man with a bald head and a shy manner, was waiting for him in the camp's old station wagon. Carl had come to town to pick up supplies and to meet Bucky's train. On shaking Carl's hand, Bucky had a single overriding thought: He's not carrying polio. And it's cool here, he realized. Even in the sun, it's cool!

Leaving town with his duffel bag stashed in the rear of the wagon, they passed along the pleasant main street of two- and three-story brick buildings— housing a row of street-level stores with business offices on the upper floors—and then turned north and began a slow ascent along zigzagging roads into the hills. They passed farms, and he saw horses and cows in the fields, and occasionally he caught sight of a farmer on a tractor. There were silos and barns and low wire fences and rural mailboxes atop wooden posts and no polio anywhere. At the top of a long climb they made a sharp turn off the blacktop onto a narrow unpaved road that was marked with a sign with the words CAMP INDIAN HILL burned into the wood and a picture below it of a teepee in a circle of flames—the same emblem that was on the side of the station wagon. After bouncing a couple of miles through the woods over the hard ridges of the dirt road—a twisting pitted track that was deliberately left that way, Carl told him, to discourage access to Indian Hill by anything other than bona fide camp traffic—they emerged into an open green oval that was the entrance to the camp grounds. Its impact was very like what he experienced upon entering Ruppert Stadium with Jake and Dave to see the Newark Bears play the first Sunday doubleheader of the season and—after stepping out from the dim stadium recesses onto the bright walkway that led to the seats—surveying the spacious sweep of mown grass secreted in one of the ugliest parts of the city. But that was a walled-in ballpark. This was the wide-open spaces. Here the vista was limitless and the refuge even more beautiful than the home field of the Bears.

A metal pole stood at the center of the oval flying an American flag and, below it, a flag bearing the camp emblem. There was also a teepee nearby, some twelve or fifteen feet high, with the long supporting poles jutting through the hole at the apex. The gray canvas was decorated at the top with two rows of a zigzag lightning-like design and near the bottom with a wavy line that must have been meant to represent a range of mountains. To either side of the teepee was a weathered totem pole.

Down the slope from the green oval was the bright metallic sheen of a vast lake. A wooden dock ran along the shoreline, and, about fifty feet from one another, three narrow wooden piers jutted out some hundred feet into the lake; at the end of two of the piers were the diving platforms. This must be the boys' waterfront that was to be his domain. Marcia had told him that the lake was fed by natural springs. The words sounded like the name of an earthly wonder: natural springs—yet another way of saying "no polio." He was wearing a white short-sleeved shirt with his tie, and stepping from the wagon, he could feel on his arms and face that, though the sun was still strong, the air here was cooler even than in Stroudsburg. As he hefted his duffel bag strap over his shoulder, he was overtaken with the joy of beginning again, the rapturous intoxication of renewal—the bursting feeling of "I live! I live!"

He followed a dirt path to a small log building overlooking the lake, where Mr. Blomback had his office. Carl had insisted on relieving Bucky of his heavy bag and driving it up to the cabin called Comanche, where he'd be living with the oldest boys in camp, the fifteen-year-olds, and their counselor. Each of the cabins in the boys' and the girls' camps was named for an Indian tribe.

He knocked on the screen door and was welcomed warmly by the owner, a tall, gangly man with a long neck and a large Adam's apple and some wisps of gray hair crisscrossing his sunburned skull. He had to have been in his late fifties, and yet, in khaki shorts and a camp polo shirt, he looked sinewy and fit. Bucky knew from Marcia that when Mr. Blomback had become a young widower in 1926, he gave up a promising scholastic career as a vice principal at Newark's West Side High and bought the camp with his wife's family money to have a place to teach his two little boys the Indian lore that he had come to love as a summer outdoorsman. The boys were grown now and off in the army, and running the camp and directing the staff and visiting Jewish families in New Jersey and Pennsylvania to recruit youngsters for the camp season was Mr. Blomback's year-round job. His rustic office—constructed of raw logs like the building's exterior—had five full Indian headdresses, arranged on pegs, decorating the wall back of the desk; group photos of campers crowded the other walls, except where there were several shelves filled with books, all, said Mr. Blomback, concerned with Indian life and lore.

"This is the bible," he told Bucky, and handed

him a thick volume called *The Book of Woodcraft*.
"This book was my inspiration. This too," and he
handed him a second and thinner book, *Manual of
the Woodcraft Indians*. Obediently Bucky thumbed
through the pages of *Manual of the Woodcraft Indians*, where he saw printed pen-and-ink drawings
of mushrooms and birds and the leaves of a great
number of trees, none of which were identifiable to
him. He saw a chapter title, "Forty Birds That Every Boy Should Know," and had to accept the fact
that he, already a man, didn't know more than a
couple of them.

"These two books have been every camp owner's inspiration," Mr. Blomback told him. "Ernest
Thompson Seton single-handedly began the Indian movement in camping. A great and influential
teacher. 'Manhood,' Seton says, 'is the first aim of
education. We follow out of doors those pursuits
that, in a word, make for manhood.' Indispensable
books. They hold up always a heroic human ideal.
They accept the red man as the great prophet of
outdoor life and woodcraft and use his methods
whenever they are helpful. They propose initia-
tion tests of fortitude, following the example of the
red man. They propose that the foundation of all

power is self-control. 'Above all,' says Seton, 'hero-ism.'"

Bucky nodded, agreeing that these were weighty matters, even if he'd never heard of Seton before.

"Every August fourteenth the camp commemorates Seton's birthday with an Indian Pageant. It's Ernest Thompson Seton who has made twentieth-century camping one of our country's greatest achievements."

Again Bucky nodded. "I'd like to read these books," he said, handing them back to Mr. Blomback. "They sound like important books, especially for educating young boys."

"At Indian Hill, educating boys *and* girls. I'd like you to read them. As soon as you get settled in, you can come and borrow my copies. Peerless books, published when the century was young and the whole nation, led by Teddy Roosevelt, was turning to the outdoor life. You are a godsend, young fellow," he said. "I've known Doc Steinberg and the Steinberg family all my life. If the Steinbergs vouch for you, that's good enough for me. I'm going to get one of the counselors to give you a tour of the camp, and I'm going to take you myself on a tour of the waterfront and introduce you to everyone there. They've all been anticipating your arrival. We have two goals at the waterfront: to teach our youngsters water skills and to teach our youngsters water safety."

"I learned the principles of both at Panzer, Mr. Blomback. I run the phys ed classes at Chancellor Avenue School with safety as my first concern."

"The parents have put their children in our care for the summer months," said Mr. Blomback. "Our job is not to fail them. We haven't had a single waterfront accident here since I bought the camp eighteen years ago. Not one."

"You can trust me, sir, to make safety foremost."

"Not a single accident," Mr. Blomback repeated sternly. "Waterfront director is one of the most responsible positions in the camp. Maybe the most responsible. A camp can be ruined by one careless accident in the water. Needless to say, every camper has a water buddy in his own grade. They must enter and leave the water together. A checkup for buddies is made before each swim and after each swim and at intervals during the swim. Lone swimming can result in fatalities."

"I think of myself as a responsible person, sir. You can rely on me to ensure the safety of every camper. Rest assured, I know about the importance of the buddy system."

"Okay, they're still serving lunch," Mr. Blomback said. "Today it's macaroni and cheese. Dinner is roast beef. Friday night is roast beef night at Indian Hill, rationing or no rationing. Come with me to the dining lodge and we'll get you something to eat. And here—here's a camp polo shirt. Take off your tie, slip it over your shirt for now, and we'll go to lunch. Irv Schlanger left his sheets, blankets, and towels. You can use them. Laundry pickup is Mondays."

The shirt was the same as the one Mr. Blomback was wearing: on the front was the name of the camp and beneath it the teepee in a circle of flames.

The dining lodge, a large timbered pavilion with open sides only steps along a wooden walkway from Mr. Blomback's lakeside office, was swarming with campers, the girls and their counselors seated at round tables on one side of the main aisle and the boys and their counselors on the other. Outside was the mild warmth of the sun—a sun that seemed benign and welcoming rather than malevolent, a nurturing Father Sun, the good god of brightness to a fecund Mother Earth—and the flickering luster

of the lake and the lush green mesh of July's growing things, about which he knew barely any more
than he knew about the birds. Inside was the noisy
clamor of children's voices reverberating in the spacious lodge, the racket that reminded him of how
much he enjoyed being around kids and why it was
he loved his work. He'd nearly forgotten what that
pleasure was like during the hard weeks of watching out for a menace against which he could offer no protection. These were happy, energetic kids
who were not imperiled by a cruel and invisible en-
emy—they could actually be shielded from mis-
hap by an adult's vigilant attention. Mercifully he
was finished with impotently witnessing terror and
death and was back in the midst of unworried children brimming with health. Here was work within
his power to accomplish.

Mr. Blomback had left him alone with his lunch,
saying they'd meet up again when Bucky had finished. In the dining lodge, nobody as yet knew or
cared who he was—kids and counselors alike were
engaged in a happy frenzy of socializing while they
ate, cabinmates talking and laughing, at some tables bursting into song, as though it weren't the
hours since breakfast but many years since they'd

been together like this. He was searching the tables for Marcia, who herself probably wasn't yet on the lookout for him. On the phone the night before, both had assumed that by the time he was settled into his cabin and got under way at the waterfront, lunch would be long over and that he'd only arrive in the dining lodge at dinnertime.

When he found her table, he was so overjoyed that he had to restrain himself from standing and shouting her name. The truth of it was that during those last three days on the playground he thought he would never see her again. From the moment he'd agreed to the Indian Hill job, he was sure he'd come down with polio and lose everything. But here she was, a strikingly dark-eyed girl with thick, curly, black-black hair that she'd had cut for the summer—there are few true blacks in nature, and Marcia's hair was one of them. Her hair had reached glamorously down to her shoulders when they first met at a faculty get-together to introduce new staff the previous fall. She appealed to him so on that first afternoon that it was a while before, face-to-face, he could look straight into her eyes or could stop himself from ogling her from afar. Then he'd seen her walking assuredly at the head of her silent class, leading her pupils through the corridors to the auditorium, and he fell for her all over again. That the kids called her Miss Steinberg mesmerized him.

Now she was deeply tanned and wearing a white camp polo shirt like his, which only enhanced the darkness of her good looks, and specifically of those eyes, whose irises struck him as not only darker but rounder than anyone else's, two dream targets, their concentric circles colored brownish black. He'd never seen her any prettier, even if she looked less like one of the counselors than like one of the campers, barely resembling the tastefully dressed first-grade teacher who already, at twenty-two, carried herself with the outward composure of an experienced professional. He noticed that her girlish little nose was dabbed with a white ointment and wondered which she was treating, sunburn or poison ivy. And then he had the most cheering thought: *That's* what you worried about up here, that's what you warned the children about—poison ivy!

There was no way to get Marcia's attention in the midst of the dining lodge hubbub. Several times he raised an arm in the air, but she did not see him, even though he held his hand aloft and waved it about. Then he saw Marcia's sisters, the Steinberg twins, Sheila and Phyllis, sitting side by side several tables away from Marcia. They were eleven now and looked entirely unlike their older sister, freckled youngsters with frizzy reddish hair and long, painfully skinny legs and noses already evolving like their father's, and both already nearly as tall as Marcia. He waved in their direction, but they were talking animatedly with the girls at their table and they didn't see him either. From the moment he'd met them he'd been completely won over by Sheila and Phyllis, their vivacity, their intelligence, their intensity, even by the ungainliness that had begun to overtake them. I am going to know these two for the rest of my life, he thought, and the prospect filled him with enormous pleasure. We will all be part of the same family. And then, all at once, he was thinking of Herbie and Alan, who had died because they'd spent the summer in Newark, and of Sheila and Phyllis, kids almost the same age who were flourishing because they were spending the summer at Indian Hill. And then there were Jake and Dave, fighting the Germans somewhere in

France while he was ensconced in this noisy fun-
house of a summer camp with all these exuberant
kids. He was struck by how lives diverge and by
how powerless each of us is up against the force of
circumstance. And where does God figure in this?
Why does He set one person down in Nazi-occupied Europe with a rifle in his hands and the other
in the Indian Hill dining lodge in front of a plate
of macaroni and cheese? Why does He place one
Weequahic child in polio-ridden Newark for the
summer and another in the splendid sanctuary of
the Poconos? For someone who had previously
found in diligence and hard work the solution to all
his problems, there was now much that was inex-
plicable to him about why what happens, happens
as it does.

"Bucky!" The twins had spotted him and, above
the din, were calling across to him. They were
standing by their table and waving their arms.
"Bucky! You made it! Hurray!"

He waved back and the twins began pointing excitedly toward where their sister was sitting.

He smiled and mouthed "I see, I see" while the
twins called to Marcia, "Bucky's here!"

Marcia stood to look around, so he stood too,

and now at last she saw him, and with both of her hands she threw him a kiss. He was saved. Polio hadn't beaten him.

HE SPENT the afternoon at the waterfront, watching as the counselors there—high school boys of seventeen, who hadn't yet reached draft age—put the campers through their swimming drills and exercises. There was nothing that wasn't familiar to him from the Teaching Swimming and Diving course he'd taken at Panzer. He looked to have inherited a beautifully run program and a perfect environment to work in—not an inch of the waterfront looked neglected, the docks, piers, platforms, and diving boards were all in superb condition, and the water was dazzlingly clear. Wooded hills thick with trees rose steeply all along the edge of the lake. The campers' cabins were tucked into low hills on the near side of the lake, the girls' camp beginning at the end of one wing of the dining lodge and the boys' at the other. About a hundred yards out there was a small wooded island covered with slanting trees whose bark appeared to be white. This must be the island where Marcia had said they could go to be safely alone.

She had managed to leave a note for him with the secretary at Mr. Blomback's office: "I couldn't believe my eyes, seeing my future husband here. I can get off at 9:30. Meet you outside the dining lodge. As the kids like to say, 'You send me.' M."

When the last of the swimming classes was over and the campers returned to their cabins to get ready for Friday night dinner and the movie that would follow, Bucky remained alone at the waterfront, delighted by how his first hours on the job had gone and elated by the company of all these unworried, wonderfully active children. He'd been in the water getting to know the counselors and how they worked and helping the kids with their strokes and their breathing, so he hadn't a chance to step out on the high board and dive. But all afternoon he'd been thinking about it, as if when he took that first dive he would be truly here.

He walked out along the narrow wooden pier that led to the high board, removed his glasses, and set them at the foot of the ladder. Then, half blind, he climbed to the board. Looking out, he could see his way to the edge of the board but distinguish little beyond that. The hills, the woods, the white island, even the lake had disappeared. He was alone on the board above the lake and could barely see a thing. The air was warm, his body was warm, and all he could hear was the pock of tennis balls being hit and the occasional clank of metal on metal where some campers off in the distance were pitching horseshoes and striking the stake. And when he breathed in, there was nothing to smell of Secaucus, New Jersey. He filled his lungs with the harmless clean air of the Pocono Mountains, then bounded three steps forward, took off, and, in control of every inch of his body throughout the blind flight, did a simple swan dive into water he could see only the instant before his arms broke neatly through and he plumbed the cold purity of the lake to its depths.

AT FIVE FORTY-FIVE, he was nearing the entrance to the dining lodge with the boys from his cabin when two campers broke away from a crowd of girls drifting in with their counselors and began calling his name. They were the Steinberg girls, twins so alike that, even up close, he had trouble telling them apart. "It's Sheila! It's Phyllis!" he cried as they hurled themselves into his arms. "You two look terrific," he said. "Look how dark you are. And you've grown again. Darn it, you're as tall as I am."

"Taller!" they shouted, squirming all over him. "Oh, don't say that," Bucky said, laughing, "please, not taller already!" "Are you going to put on a diving exhibition?" one of them said. "Nobody's asked me to so far," he replied. "We're asking you to! A diving exhibition for the whole camp! All those twisting and backward things that you do in the air."

The girls had seen him dive a couple of months back, when he'd been invited down the shore to the Steinbergs' summer home in Deal for the Memorial Day weekend, and they'd all gone together to the swim club at the beach where the Steinbergs were members. It was the first time he'd been an overnight guest of the family's, and once he'd put aside his jitters about what someone of his background might talk about with such educated people, he found that Marcia's mother and father couldn't have been more kind and companionable. He remembered the pleasure he had taken in giving the twins basic instruction, at the low board of the swimming pool, on balancing themselves and taking off. They were timid to begin with, but by the end of the afternoon he had them doing straight dives off the board. By then he was their matinee idol, and they would wrest him from their older sister at every opportunity. And he was taken with them, the girls Dr. Steinberg appreciatively referred to as his "identically sparkling duo."

"I missed you two," he said to the twins. "Are you staying for the rest of the summer?" they asked. "I sure am." "Because Mr. Schlanger went into the army?" "That's right." "That's what Marcia said, but at first we thought she was dreaming." "I think I'm dreaming, being here," Bucky replied. "I'll see you girls later," he said, and, showing off for their cabinmates, they each lifted their faces to kiss him demonstratively on the lips. And, as they ran for the dining lodge entrance, no less demonstratively, they called, "We love you, Bucky!"

He ate next to the Comanche cabin counselor, Donald Kaplow, a seventeen-year-old who was a track-and-field enthusiast and threw the discus for his high school. When Bucky told him that he threw the javelin, Donald said that he had brought his equipment with him to camp, and whenever he had time off he practiced his throws in an open hayfield back of the girls' camp, where they held the big Indian Pageant in August. He wondered if Bucky would come along sometime to watch and give him some pointers. "Sure, sure," said Bucky.

"I watched you this afternoon," Donald said. "From the porch of our cabin you can see the lake. I watched you dive. Are you a competitive diver?"

"I can do the elementary competitive dives, but, no, I'm not a competitor."

"I never got my dives down. I repeat all kinds of ridiculous mistakes."

"Maybe I can help," Bucky said.

"Would you?"

"If there's time, sure."

"Oh, that's great. Thanks."

"We'll take them one by one. All you probably need are a few faults corrected and you'll be fine."

"And I'm not hogging your time?"

"Nope. If and when I have the time, it's yours."

"Thanks again, Mr. Cantor."

When he looked over to the girls' side of the dining lodge to see if he could find Marcia, he caught the eye of one of the Steinberg twins, who frantically waved her arm at him. He smiled and waved back and realized that in less than a day he had rid himself of his polio thoughts, except for a few minutes earlier, when he was reminded by Donald of Alan Michaels. Though Donald was five years older and already six feet tall, they were both nice-look-ing boys with broad shoulders and lean frames and long, strong legs, both avid to latch on to an in-structor who could help them improve themselves at sports. Boys like Alan and Donald, seeming to sense right off the depth of his devotion to teaching and his capacity to give them assurance where they needed it, were quickly drawn into his mentoring orbit. Had Alan lived, he more than likely would have grown into an adolescent much like Donald Kaplow. Had Alan lived, had Herbie Steinmark lived, Bucky more than likely wouldn't be here and the unimaginable wouldn't be happening at home.

He and marcia canoed across the lake—he'd never been in a canoe before, but Marcia showed him how to handle the paddle, and watching her, he picked it up after only a few strokes. They moved slowly into the dark, and when they reached the narrow island, which was far longer than he'd real-ized at the boys' waterfront, they steered around to the far side, where they dragged the canoe ashore and pulled it back into a small grove of trees. They had hardly spoken from the time they touched hands outside the dining lodge and hurried over to the girls' waterfront to silently lift a canoe from the rack there.

There was no moon, no stars, no light except from a few of the cabins on the hillside back on shore. There had been the roast beef dinner in the dining lodge—where Donald Kaplow, with a boy's voracious appetite, had downed slice after slice of juicy red meat—and now there was a movie playing in the rec hall for the older kids, so the only sound that carried from the camp was the distant noise of the movie track. Close by they could hear the orchestral thrumming of frogs, and from far away a long rumble of thunder was audible every few minutes. The drama of the thunder didn't make their being alone together on the wooded island in their khaki shorts and camp polo shirts any less momentous or diminish the stimulus of their scanty clothes. Their arms and legs bare, they stood in a little cleared patch in among the trees, the two so close to each other that he could plainly see her despite the dark. Marcia, on her own, had gone out in the canoe and prepared the clearing a few nights earlier, readying the spot for their rendezvous by using her hands to rake away the leaves that had piled up the previous fall.

All around them the island was thickly packed with clusters of trees, which weren't entirely white, as they had looked to him from the waterfront, but bore black slashes encircling their bark as though they'd been scarred by a whip. The trunks of a number of them were bent or broken, some growing almost doubled over, some jaggedly torn apart halfway to the ground, some completely sheared off, ravaged by the weather or disease. The trees still intact were so elegantly slender that he could have wrapped his fingers around any one of them with as little difficulty as when he playfully clasped one of Marcia's thighs in the ring of his ten strong fingers. The upper branches and drooping branchlets of the undamaged trees spanned the clearing, creating a latticed dome of saw-toothed leaves and delicately thin, overarching limbs. It was a perfect hideaway, sequestration such as they could only dream about while, necking heavily on the Steinbergs' front porch, they attempted to muffle those readily identifiable noises that signal arousal, intense pleasure, and climax.

"What do you call these trees?" he asked, putting his hand out to touch one. All at once, he had become inexplicably shy, just as when they had been introduced at that first faculty get-together and he found himself moving woodenly and with a ridiculously unnatural expression on his face. She had surprised him by extending her little hand to shake, and he was so befuddled that he wasn't sure what to do with it—the allure of her petite figure left him unable even to think of how to address her. The encounter had been colossally embarrassing for someone whose grandfather had raised him to believe that he must consider nothing beyond his strength to undertake, least of all saying hello to a girl who probably didn't weigh a hundred pounds.

"Birches," she answered. "They're white birches —silver birches."

"Some of the bark is peeling away." He easily stripped a swatch of thin silvery bark from the tree trunk under his hand and showed it to her, there in the dark, as though they were children on a nature hike.

"The Indians used birch bark for canoes," she told him.

"Of course," he said. "Birch bark canoes. I never thought it was the name of a tree."

There was silence between them while they listened to the mumble of the movie voices floating over the water and the thunder far away and the frogs nearby and the thud of something across the lake knocking against the swimming dock or the piers. His heartbeat quickened when he realized it could be Mr. Blomback, coming after them in another canoe.

"Why are there no birds out here?" he asked finally.

"There are. Birds don't sing at night."

"Don't or do?"

"Oh, Bucky," she whispered beseechingly, "must we really go on like this? Undress me, please. Undress me now."

After their weeks of separation, he had needed her to tell him that. He needed this intelligent girl to tell him everything, really, about life beyond the playground and the athletic field and the gym. He needed her entire family to tell him how to live a grown man's life in all the ways that nobody, including his grandfather, had yet done.

Instantly he undid the belt and the buttons on her shorts and slid them down over her legs to the ground. Meanwhile, she raised her arms like a child, and first he took the flashlight she was carrying out of her hand and then he gently pulled the polo shirt off over her head. She reached around to unhook her bra while he knelt and, with the bizarre, somewhat shaming sensation that he had lived for this moment, pulled her underpants down her legs and off over her feet.

"My socks," she said, having already kicked off her sneakers. He pulled off her socks and stuffed them into the sneakers. The socks were spotless and white and, along with the rest of what she was wearing, faintly fragrant of bleach from the camp laundry.

Without her clothes, she was small and slim, with beautifully formed, lightly muscled legs and thin arms and fragile wrists and tiny breasts, affixed high on her chest, and nipples that were soft, pale, and unprotuberant. The slender elfin female body looked as vulnerable as a child's. She certainly didn't look like someone familiar with copulation, nor was that far from the truth. One late-fall weekend when the rest of her family was away in Deal and when, at

about four on a Saturday afternoon, with the shades
pulled down in her bedroom on Goldsmith Avenue,
he had taken her virginity—and lost his own—she
had whispered to him afterward, "Bucky, teach me
about sex," as if of the two of them she were the less
experienced. They lay together on the bed for hours
after that—*her* bed, he had thought, the very four-
poster with carved posts and a flowered chintz canopy and a ruffled skirt in which she had been sleeping since childhood—while she, in a soft confiding
voice, as though there were indeed others in the
empty house, spoke of her unbelievable good luck
in having not just her wonderful family but Bucky
to love too. He then told her more than he ever had
before about his boyhood, expressing himself more
easily with her than he had with any girl he'd ever
known, with *anyone* he'd ever known, revealing all
he normally kept to himself about what made him
happy and what made him sad. "I was the son of a
thief," he admitted and found himself able to speak
these words to her without a trace of shame. "He
went to jail for stealing money. He's an ex-convict.
I've never seen him. I don't know where he lives,
or even if he's alive or dead. If he had raised me,
who's to know if I wouldn't have turned out to be

a thief myself? On my own, without grandparents like mine, in a neighborhood like mine," he told her, "it wouldn't have been hard to end up a bum."

Lying face-to-face in the four-poster, they went on with their stories until it was dusk, then dark, until both had said just about everything and revealed themselves to each other as fully as they knew how. And then, as if he weren't sufficiently captivated by her, Marcia whispered into his ear something she had just then learned. "This is the only way to talk, isn't it?"

"You," MARCIA WHISPERED after he'd undressed her. "Now you."

Quickly he pulled off his things and set them down next to hers at the edge of their clearing.

"Let me look at you. Oh, thank God," she said and burst into tears. He quickly gathered her into his arms, but it did not help. She sobbed without restraint.

"What is it?" he asked her. "What's the matter?"

"I thought you were going to die!" she exclaimed. "I thought you were going to become paralyzed and die! I couldn't sleep, I was so frightened. I'd come out here whenever I could to be alone and pray to God to keep you healthy. I never prayed so hard for anyone in my life. 'Please protect Bucky!' I'm crying like this out of happiness, darling! Such great, great happiness! You're here! You didn't get it! Oh, Bucky, hold me tight, hold me as close as you can! You're safe!"

WHEN THEY WERE dressed and ready to return to camp, he could not help himself and instead of chalking up her words to how relieved she was and forgetting them, he said what he shouldn't have said about her praying to the god whom he had repudiated. He knew there was no good reason to conclude this momentous day by returning to a subject so inflammatory, especially as he'd never heard her speak like that before and probably wouldn't ever again. It was a subject entirely too grave for the moment, and irrelevant, really, now that he was here. Yet he could not restrain himself. He'd been through too much back in Newark to squelch his feelings—and he'd left Newark and its pestilence a mere twelve hours ago.

"Do you really think God answered your prayers?" he asked her.

"I can't really know, can I? But you're here, aren't you? You're healthy, aren't you?"

"That doesn't prove anything," he said. "Why didn't God answer the prayers of Alan Michaels's parents? They must have prayed. Herbie Steinmark's parents must have prayed. They're good people. They're good Jews. Why didn't God intervene for them? Why didn't He save their boys?"

"I honestly don't know," Marcia helplessly answered.

"I don't either. I don't know why God created polio in the first place. What was He trying to prove? That we need people on earth who are crippled?"

"God didn't create polio," she said.

"You think not?"

"Yes," she said sharply, "I think not."

"But didn't God create everything?"

"That isn't the same thing."

"Why isn't it?"

"Why are you arguing with me, Bucky? What are we arguing *for*? All I said was that I prayed to God because I was frightened for you. And now you're here and I'm overwhelmingly happy. And out of that you've made an argument. Why do you want to fight with me when we haven't seen each other for weeks?"

"I don't want to fight," he said.

"Then don't," she said, more bewildered than angry.

All this while the thunder had been rolling in regularly and the lightning flickering nearby.

"We should go," she said. "We should get back while the storm is still a way off."

"But how can a Jew pray to a god who has put a curse like this on a neighborhood of thousands and thousands of Jews?"

"I don't know! What exactly are you driving at?"

He was suddenly afraid to tell her—afraid that if he persisted in pressing her to understand what he did, he would lose her and the family with her. They had never before argued or clashed over anything. Never once had he sensed in his loving Marcia a speck of opposition—or she in him, for that matter—and so, just in time, before he began to ruin things, Bucky reined himself in.

Together they dragged the canoe down to the edge of the lake, and within moments, without speaking, they were vigorously paddling toward camp and arrived well before the downpour began.

DONALD KAPLOW AND the other boys were asleep when Bucky entered the Comanche cabin and made his way down the narrow aisle between the footlockers. Quietly as he could, he got into his pajamas, stowed away his clothes, and slid between the fresh sheets that formerly belonged to Irv Schlanger and that he'd made the bed with earlier in the day. He and Marcia had not parted pleasantly, and he continued to feel the distress from when they'd hurriedly kissed good night at the landing and, each fearing that something other than God might lie at the root of their first quarrel, had run off in opposite directions for their cabins.

The rain began pounding on the cabin roof while Bucky lay awake thinking about Dave and Jake fighting in France in a war from which he'd been excluded. He thought of Irv Schlanger, the draftee who'd gone off to war after having slept only the night before in this very bed. Time and again it seemed as if everybody had gone off to war except him. To have been preserved from the fighting, to have escaped the bloodshed—all that someone else

might have considered a boon, he saw as an afflic-
tion. He was raised to be a fearless battler by his
grandfather, trained to think he must be a hugely
responsible man, ready and fit to defend what was
right, and instead, confronted with the struggle of
the century, a worldwide conflict between good and
evil, he could not take even the smallest part.

Yet he *had* been given a war to fight, the war being waged on the battlefield of his playground, the
war whose troops he had deserted for Marcia and
the safety of Indian Hill. If he could not fight in Europe or the Pacific, he could at least have remained
in Newark, fighting their fear of polio alongside his
endangered boys. Instead he was here in this haven
devoid of danger; instead he had chosen to leave
Newark for a summer camp atop a secluded mountain, concealed from the world at the far end of a
narrow unpaved road and camouflaged from the air
by a forest of trees—and doing what there? Playing
with children. And happy at it! And the happier he
felt, the more humiliating it was.

Despite the heavy rain drilling on the cabin roof
and turning the grassy playing fields and the worn
dirt trails into an enormous soggy puddle, despite
the boom of thunder reverberating through the

range of mountains and lightning jaggedly branching downward all around the camp, none of the boys in the two rows of bunks so much as stirred in their sleep. This simple, cozy log cabin—with its colorful school pennants and its decorated canoe paddles and its sticker-laden footlockers and its narrow camp beds with shoes, sneakers, and sandals lined up beneath them, with its securely sleeping crew of robust, healthy teenage boys—seemed as far from war, from *his* war, as he could have gotten. Here he had the innocent love of his two future sisters-in-law and the passionate love of his future wife; here he already had a boy like Donald Kaplow eagerly seeking instruction from him; here he had a marvelous waterfront to preside over and dozens of energetic youngsters to teach and encourage; here, at the end of the day, he had the high board to dive from in peace and tranquillity. Here he was shielded by as secure a refuge as you could find from the killer on the rampage at home. Here he had everything that Dave and Jake were without and that the kids on the Chancellor playground were without and that everyone in Newark was without. But what he no longer had was a conscience he could live with.

He would have to go back. Tomorrow he would have to take a train from Stroudsburg and, once back in Newark, make contact with O'Gara and tell him he wanted to resume work at the playground on Monday. Since the recreation department was short-handed because of the draft, there should be no problem recovering his job. In all, he would have been gone from the playground for a day and a half—and no one could say that a day and half off in the Poconos constituted negligence or desertion.

But wouldn't Marcia take his returning to Newark as a blow, as somehow castigating her, especially since their evening on the island had ended unhappily? If he picked up and left tomorrow, what repercussions would that have for their plans? He already intended to go into town as soon as he had an hour free and, with the fifty dollars he'd drawn out of the savings account for his grandmother's stove, buy Marcia an engagement ring at the local jewelry store . . . But he could not worry—not about Marcia's ring, not about Marcia's misunderstanding why he was going, not about leaving Mr. Blomback in the lurch, not about disappointing Donald Kaplow or the Steinberg twins. He had made a profound mistake. Rashly, he had yielded to fear, and under the spell of fear he had betrayed his boys and betrayed himself, when all he'd had to do was stay where he was and do his job. Marcia's lovingly trying to rescue him from Newark had led to his foolishly undermining himself. The kids here would do fine without him. This was no war zone. Indian Hill was where he *wasn't* needed.

Outside, just when it seemed it could not come down any harder, the rain reached a startling crescendo and began gushing like floodwater down the cabin's pitched roof and over the brimming gutters and sweeping past the closed windows in plummeting sheets. Suppose it were to rain like this in Newark, suppose it were to rain there for days on end, millions and millions of water drops slashing the houses and alleyways and streets of the city—would that wash the polio away? But why speculate about what was not and could not be? He had to head home! His impulse was to get up and pack his belongings in his duffel bag so as to be ready to catch the first morning train. But he didn't want to wake the boys or make it look as if he were rushing off in a panic. It was his rushing here that had been undertaken in a panic. He was leaving after hav-

ing recovered his courage for an ordeal whose re-
ality was undeniable, yet an ordeal whose hazards
couldn't compare to those that threatened Dave
and Jake as they battled to extend the Allied foot-
hold in France.

As for God, it was easy to think kindly of Him in
a paradise like Indian Hill. It was something else in
Newark—or Europe or the Pacific—in the summer
of 1944.

BY THE NEXT MORNING the wet world of the storm
had vanished, and the sun was too brilliant, the
weather too invigorating, the high excitement of
the boys beginning their new day unfettered by fear
too inspiring for him to imagine never awakening
again within these cabin walls plastered with pennants from a dozen schools. And jeopardizing their
future by precipitously abandoning Marcia was too
horrifying to contemplate. The view from the cabin
porch of the ripple-free gloss of the lake into which
he had dived so deeply at the end of his first day
and, in the distance, of the island where they had
canoed to make love beneath the canopy of birch
leaves—to divest himself of this after just one day
was impossible. He was even fortified by the sight

of the soaked floorboards at the entrance to the cabin, where the wind had whipped the raindrops across the porch and through the screen door— even that ordinary marker of a torrential downpour somehow sustained him in his decision to stay. Under a sky scoured to an eggshell smoothness by that driving storm, with birds calling and flying about overhead, and in the company of all these exhilarated kids, how could he do otherwise? He wasn't a doctor. He wasn't a nurse. He could not return to a tragedy whose conditions he was impotent to change.

Forget about God, he told himself. Since when is God your business anyway? And, enacting the role that was his business, he headed off for breakfast with the boys, filling his lungs with fresh mountain air purified of all contaminants. While they trooped across the grassy slope of the hill, a rich moist green smell, brand new to him, rose from the rain-soaked earth and seemed to certify that he was indisputably in tune with life. He had always lived in a city flat with his grandparents and had never before felt on his skin that commingling of warmth and coolness that is a July mountain morning, or known the fullness of emotion it could excite. There was something so enlivening about spending one's workday in this unbounded space, something so beguiling about stripping Marcia of her clothes in the dark of an empty island apart from everyone, something so thrilling about going to sleep beneath a blitz-krieg of thunder and lightning and awakening to what looked like the first morning ever that the sun had shone down on human activity. I'm here, he thought, and I'm happy—and so he was, cheered even by the squishing sound made by tramping on the sodden grass cushioning his every step. It's all here! Peace! Love! Health! Beauty! Children! Work! What else was there to do but stay? Yes, everything he saw and smelled and heard was a telling premonition of that phantom, future happiness.

Later in the day there was an unusual incident, one said never to have occurred at the camp before. A huge swarm of butterflies settled over Indian Hill, and for about an hour in the middle of the afternoon they could be seen erratically dipping and darting over the playing fields and thickly perched on the tape of the tennis nets and alighting on the clusters of milkweed growing plentifully at the fringe of the camp grounds. Had they been blown in overnight on the strong storm winds? Had they lost their way while migrating south? But why would they be migrating so early in the summer? Nobody, not even the nature counselor, knew the answer. They appeared en masse as if to scrutinize every blade of grass, every shrub, every tree, every vine stem, fern frond, weed, and flower petal in the mountaintop camp before reorienting themselves to resume their flight to wherever it was they were headed.

While he stood in the hot sun at the dock, watching the faces full of sunlight bobbing about in the water, one of the butterflies landed on Bucky and began to sip on his bare shoulder. Miraculous! Imbibing the minerals of his perspiration! Fantastic! Bucky remained motionless, observing the butterfly out of the corner of his eye until the thing levitated and was suddenly gone. Later, recounting the episode to the boys in the cabin, he told them that his butterfly looked as though it had been designed and painted by the Indians, with its veined wings patterned in orange and black and the black edging minutely dotted with tiny white spots—what he did not tell them was that he was so astonished by the gorgeous butterfly's feeding on his flesh that when it flew off he allowed himself to half believe that this too must be an omen of bounteous days to come.

Nobody at Indian Hill was afraid of the butter-flies blanketing the camp and brightly clouding the air. Rather, everyone smiled with delight at all that silent, spirited flitting about, campers and counsel-ors alike thrilled to feel themselves engulfed by the weightless fragility of those innumerable, colorful fluttering wings. Some campers came racing out of their cabins wielding butterfly nets that they'd made in crafts, and the youngest children ran madly after the rising, plunging butterflies, trying to catch them with their outstretched hands. Everybody was happy, because everybody knew that butterflies didn't bite or spread disease but disseminated the pollen that made seed plants grow. What could be more salutary than that?

Yes, the playground in Newark was behind him. He would not leave Indian Hill. There he was prey to polio; here he was food for butterflies. Vacilla-tion—a painful weakness previously unknown to him—would no longer subvert his assurance of what needed to be done.

*

BY THIS POINT in the summer, the beginners in the boys' camp had progressed beyond blowing bubbles in the water and practicing the face-down float and were at least swimming the dog paddle; many were beyond that, well into the elementary backstroke and crawl, and a few of the beginners were already jumping into the deep water and swimming twenty feet to the shallow edge of the lake. He had five counselors on his staff, and though they seemed adept at handling boys of all ages and at conducting the swimming program under his supervision, Bucky found himself, from the first day, drawn into the water to work with what the counselors privately called the "sinkers," the young ones who were least sure of themselves and making the slowest progress and who seemed lacking in natural buoyancy. He would walk out along the pier to the deep-water platform where a counselor was instructing the older boys in diving; he would spend time with kids who were working hard to improve their butterfly stroke; but invariably he would return to the young ones and get down into the water with them and work on their flutter kick and their scissors kick and their frog kick, reassuring them with the support of his hands and just a few words that he was right there and they were in no danger of choking on a mouthful of water, let alone of drowning. By the end of a day at the waterfront he thought, exactly as he had when he began at Panzer, that there could be no more satisfying job for a man than giving a boy learning a sport, along with the basic instruction, the security and confidence that all will be well and getting him over the fear of a new experience, whether it was in swimming or boxing or baseball.

A matchless day, with dozens to come. Before dinner he'd get his wettish welcome on the lips from the twins, who'd be waiting for him at the dining lodge steps and who sent up a cry of "Kiss! Kiss!" the moment he came into sight, and after dinner he had promised Donald Kaplow he would work with him on his dives. Then, at nine-thirty, off to the dark island with his wife-to-be. She'd left another note in an envelope at Mr. Blomback's office. "More. Meet me. M." He had already arranged with Carl to drive him into Stroudsburg during the week so he could buy Marcia's engagement ring.

About half an hour after dinner, while the boys from their cabin played in a pickup softball game on the diamond by the flagpole, he and Donald went down to the dock for Bucky to watch Donald's springboard dives. Donald started off with a front dive, a back dive, and a front jackknife.

"Good!" Bucky said to him. "I don't understand what you think is wrong with them."

Donald smiled at the compliment but asked anyway, "Is my approach right? Is my hurdle right?"

"You bet they are," Bucky said. "You know what you want to do and you do it. You do a model jackknife. First the upper part of the body bends over and the legs do nothing. Then the lower part of the body comes up behind while the head and arms are stable. Right in every detail. Do you do a back somersault? Let's see it. Watch out for the board."

Donald was a natural diver and didn't exhibit a single one of the faults that Bucky might have expected to see in the back somersault. When Donald came up from the dive and was still in the water pushing the hair out of his eyes, Bucky called to him, "Good forceful spin. You keep the tuck nice and tight. Timing, balance—great job all around."

Donald climbed out of the water onto the dock, and when Bucky tossed him a towel, he rubbed himself dry. "Is it too chilly out here for you?" Bucky asked. "Are you cold?"

"No, not at all," Donald answered.

The sun was still radiant and the big sky still blue but the temperature had dropped close to ten degrees since dinner. Hard to believe that only days earlier he and his playground boys had been suffering the very heat that incubated the pestilence that was ravaging his city and making people crazy with fear. And dizzying to realize that up here every last thing had changed for the better. If only the temperature in Newark could drop like this and stay like this for the rest of July and August!

"You're shivering," Bucky said. "Let's pick up again same time tomorrow. How about it?"

"But just the forward somersault, please? I'll do it first from the end of the board," Donald said, and he took up his position with his arms in front, his elbows flexed, and his knees slightly bent. "This isn't my best dive," he said.

"Concentrate," Bucky said. "Upward arm lift and then tuck."

Donald readied himself and then dived forward and up, rolled into the tuck, and came down feet-first, making a classic vertical entry into the lake.

"Did I screw up?" Donald asked when he surfaced. He had to shade his eyes from the western sun and the sparkling glare it threw across the water in order to see Bucky clearly.

"Nope," Bucky told him. "Momentarily your hands lost contact with your legs, but that didn't matter much."

"Didn't it? Let me do it again," he said, breast-stroking up to the ladder. "Let me get it right."

"Okay, Ace," Bucky said, laughing, and pinning on Donald the nickname he'd been dubbed with on the street as a little kid with pointy ears, back before his grandfather had stepped in to rename him for good. "One last forward somersault and we go inside."

This time, starting from the foot of the board, Donald began with his regular approach and takeoff and expertly completed the dive. His hands moved faultlessly from his shins to the sides of his knees and then to the sides of his thighs in the break.

"Great!" Bucky called to him as he emerged at the surface. "Great height, great spin. Nice and forceful from beginning to end. Where are all those mistakes you told me you make? You don't make any."

"Mr. Cantor," he said excitedly as he climbed back onto the dock, "let me show you my half twist and my back jackknife and then we'll go in. Let me finish the sequence. I'm not cold, really."

"But I am," Bucky said, laughing, "and I'm dry and have a shirt on."

"Well," replied Donald, "that's the difference between seventeen and twenty-four."

"Twenty-three," said Bucky, laughing again and as pleased as he could be—pleased by Donald and his perseverance and filled with contentment knowing that Marcia and the twins were only steps away. It was almost as if they were a family already. As if Donald, only six years his junior, were Marcia's and his own son and, incongruously, the twins' nephew. "Look," he said, "the temperature is going down by the minute. We've got the whole rest of the summer to practice out here." And he tossed Donald his sweatshirt to put on and, for good measure, had him wrap the towel around the waist of his wet trunks.

On the trudge up the slope to the cabin, Donald said, "I want to join the naval air corps when I'm eighteen. My best friend went in a year ago. We write all the time. He told me about the training. It's tough. But I want to get into the war before it ends. I want to fly against the Japs. I've wanted to since Pearl Harbor. I was fourteen when the war began, old enough to know what was happening and to want to do something about it. I want to be in on it when the Japs surrender. What a day that's going to be."

"I hope you get the chance," Bucky told him.

"What kept you out, Mr. Cantor?"

"My eyesight. These things." He tapped his glasses with a fingernail. "I've got my closest buddies fighting in France. They jumped into Normandy on D-Day. I wish I could have been with them."

"I follow the war in the Pacific," Donald said. "In Europe it's going to be quick now. This is the beginning of the end for Germany. But in the Pacific there's still plenty of fighting to be done. Last month, in the Marianas, we destroyed one hundred forty Jap planes in two days. Imagine being in on that."

"There's plenty of fighting left on both fronts," Bucky told him. "You won't miss out."

As they mounted the Comanche cabin steps, Donald asked, "Can you watch the rest of the dives after dinner tomorrow night?"

"Sure I can."

"And thanks, Mr. Cantor, for giving me all that time."

And there on the cabin porch, Donald reached out a bit stiffly to shake his hand—a surprising formality with its own ingratiating appeal. One session at the diving board and already they were like old friends, though while standing there with Donald at the end of a beautiful summer day, Bucky was unexpectedly stung by the thought of all the boys he'd abandoned on the playground. Try as he would to take delight in everything here, he couldn't yet succeed entirely in shutting out the inexcusable act and the place where he was no longer esteemed.

BETWEEN THE TIME that he left Donald and had arranged to meet Marcia, he went to the phone booth back of the camp office to call his grandmother. Probably he wasn't going to catch her in, because she would be sitting outside on a beach chair with the Einnemans and the Fishers, but as it happened, though the heat was supposed to return again the next day, the city had cooled off for twenty-four hours and she was able to sit in their flat with the windows open and the fan on and to listen to her programs on the radio. She asked how he was and how Marcia and the twins were, and when he told her that he and Marcia were getting engaged, she said, "I don't know whether to laugh or cry. My Eugene."

"Laugh," he said, laughing.

"Yes, I'm happy for you, darling," she said, "but I wish your mother had lived to see this. I only wish she had lived to see the man her son turned out to be. I wish Grandpa could be here. He would be excited for his boy. So proud. Dr. Steinberg's daughter."

"I wish he could be here too, Grandma. I think about him up here," Bucky said. "I thought about him yesterday when I went off the high board. I remembered how he taught me to swim at the Y. I was about six. He threw me into the pool and that was it. How are you, Grandma? Are the Einnemans looking after you all right?"

"Of course they are. Don't you worry about me. The Einnemans are very helpful, and I can take care of myself anyway. Eugene, I have to tell you something. There have been thirty new cases of polio in the Weequahic section. Seventy-nine in the city in just the last day. Nineteen dead. All records. And there have been more cases of polio at the Chancellor playground. Selma Shankman called me. She told me the boys' names and I wrote them down."

"Who are they, Grandma?"

"Let me get my glasses. Let me get the piece of paper," she said.

Several counselors were now standing in line outside the booth waiting to use the phone, and he signaled to them through the glass that he would be only another few minutes. Meanwhile, he waited in dread to hear the names. Why cripple children, he thought. Why a disease that cripples children? Why destroy our irreplaceable children? They're the best kids in the world.

"Eugene?"

"I'm here."

"All right. These are the names. These are the boys who are hospitalized. Billy Schizer and Erwin Frankel. And one death."

"Who died?

"A boy named Ronald Graubard. He got sick and died overnight. Did you know him?"

"I know him, Grandma, yes. I know him from the playground and from school. I know them all. Ronnie is dead. I can't believe it."

"I'm sorry to have to tell you," his grandmother said, "but I thought, because you were so close to all those boys, you would want to know."

"You were right. Of course I want to know."

"There are people in the city who are calling for a quarantine of the Weequahic section. There's talk from the mayor's office about a quarantine," she told him.

"A quarantine of all of Weequahic?"

"Yes. Barricading it off so nobody can go in or out. They would close it off at the Irvington line and the Hillside line and then at Hawthorne Avenue and at Elizabeth Avenue. That's what it said in tonight's paper. They even printed a map."

"But there are tens of thousands of people there, people who have jobs and have to go to work. They can't just pen people in like that, can they?"

"Things are bad, Eugene. People are up in arms. People are terrified. Everybody is frightened for their children. Thank God you're away. The bus drivers on the eight and fourteen lines say they won't drive into the Weequahic section unless they have protective masks. Some say they won't drive in there at all. The mailmen don't want to deliver mail there. The truck drivers who transport supplies to the stores, to the groceries, to the gas stations, and so on don't want to go in either. Strangers drive through with their windows rolled up no matter how hot it is outside. The anti-Semites are saying that it's because they're Jews that polio spreads there. Because of all the Jews—that's why Weequahic is the center of the paralysis and why the Jews should be isolated. Some of them sound as if they think the best way to get rid of the polio epidemic would be to burn down Weequahic with all the Jews in it. There is a lot of bad feeling because of the crazy things people are saying out of their fear. Out of their fear and out of their hatred. I was born in the city, and I've never known anything like this in my life. It's as if everything everywhere is collapsing."

"Yes, it sounds very bad," he said, dropping the last of his coins into the phone.

"And, Eugene, of course—I almost forgot. They're shutting down the playgrounds. As of tomorrow. Not just Chancellor but all over the city."

"They are? But the mayor was set on keeping them open."

"It's in tonight's paper. All the places where children congregate are being shut down. I have the article in front of me. Movie theaters are shutting down for children under sixteen. The city pool is shutting down. The public library with all its branches is shutting down. Pastors are shutting down Sunday schools. It's all in the paper. Schools might not open on schedule if things continue like this. I'll read you the opening line. 'There is a possibility that the public schools—'"

"But what does it say specifically about the playgrounds?"

"Nothing. It's just in a list of things that the mayor is now closing."

So if he'd remained in Newark a few days longer, he would never have had to quit. Instead he would have been released, free to do whatever he wanted and to go wherever he liked. If only he'd stayed, he would never have had to phone O'Gara and take what he took from O'Gara. If only he'd stayed, he would never have had to walk out on his kids and look back for a lifetime at his inexcusable act.

"Here. Here's the headline," she said. "'Day's Record in City Polio Cases. Mayor Closes Facilities.' Should I send you the article, darling? Should I tear it out?"

"No, no. Grandma, there are counselors waiting

to use the phone and I don't have more change anyway. I have to go. Goodbye for now."

MARCIA WAS WAITING by the entrance to the dining lodge, and together, wearing heavy sweaters against the unseasonable cold, they slipped down to the waterfront, where they found the canoe and started off across the lake through a rising mist, the silence broken only by the slurp of the paddle blades dipping into the water. At the island they paddled around to the far side and dragged the canoe ashore. Marcia had brought a blanket. He helped her to shake it open and spread it in the clearing.

"What's happened?" she asked. "What's the matter?"

"News from my grandmother. Seventy-nine new cases in Newark overnight. Thirty new cases at Weequahic. Three new cases at the playground. Two hospitalized and one dead. Ronnie Graubard. A quick, bright little fellow, full of spark, and he's dead."

Marcia took his hand. "I don't know what to say, Bucky. It's dreadful."

He sat down on the blanket and she sat beside him. "I don't know what to say either," he told her.

"Isn't it time for them to close the playground?" she asked.

"They have. They've closed it. They've closed all the playgrounds."

"When?"

"As of tomorrow. The mayor's shutting them down, my grandmother said."

"Well, wasn't that the best thing to do? He should have done it a long time ago."

"I should have stayed, Marcia. For as long as the playground was open, I should never have left."

"But it was only the other day that you got here."

"I left. There's nothing more to say. A fact is a fact. I left."

He drew her close to him on the blanket. "Here," he said. "Lie here with me," and he pressed her body to his. They held each other without speaking. There was nothing more that he knew of to say or to think. He had left while all the boys had stayed, and now two more of them were sick and one was dead.

"Is this what you've been thinking about since you got here? That you left?"

"If I were in Newark I would go to Ronnie's funeral. If I were in Newark I would visit the families. Instead I'm here."

"You can still do that when you get back."

"That's not the same thing."

"But even if you had stayed, what could you have done?"

"It isn't a matter of *doing*—it's a matter of being there! I should be there now, Marcia! Instead I'm at the top of a mountain in the middle of a lake!"

They held each other without speaking. Fifteen minutes must have passed. All Bucky could think of were their names, and all he could see were their faces: Billy Schizer. Ronald Graubard. Danny Kopferman. Myron Kopferman. Alan Michaels. Erwin Frankel. Herbie Steinmark. Leo Feinswog. Paul Lippman. Arnie Mesnikoff. All he could think of was the war in Newark and the boys that he had fled.

Another fifteen minutes must have passed before Marcia spoke again. In a hushed voice she said to him, "The stars are breathtaking. You never see stars like this at home. I'll bet this is the first time you've ever seen a night sky so full of stars."

He said nothing.

"Look," she said, "how when the leaves move

they let the starlight through. And the sun," she said a moment later, "did you see the sun this evening just as it was beginning to go down? It seemed so close to camp. Like a gong you could reach out and strike. All that's up there is so vast," she said, still vainly, naively trying to stop him from feeling unworthy, "and we are infinitesimal."

Yes, he thought, and there's something more infinitesimal than us. The virus destroying everything.

"Listen," Marcia said. "Shhh. Hear that?" There had been a social at the rec hall earlier in the evening, and the campers who had stayed behind to clean up must have put a record on the record player to keep them company while they gathered up soda bottles and swept the floor and the rest of the kids went off with their counselors to get ready for lights out. Over the silence of the dark lake came Marcia's favorite song of the summer. It was the song that was playing on the jukebox at Syd's the day Bucky had gone to extend his condolences to Alan's family, the same day he'd learned from Yushy the counterman that Herbie had died too.

"'I'll be seeing you,'" Marcia sang to him softly, "'in all the old familiar places—'" And here she stood, pulled him after her, and, determined not to let his spirits drop any further—and not knowing what else to do—she got him to begin to dance.

"'That this heart of mine embraces,'" she sang, her cheek pressed to his chest, "'all day through . . .'" And her voice rose appealingly on the elongated "through."

He did as she wanted and obligingly held her to him and, shuffling her slowly around the middle of the clearing that they had made their own, remembered the night before she'd left for Indian Hill at the end of June, when they'd danced together just like this to the radio music on her family's porch. It was a night when all they'd had to be concerned about was Marcia's going away for the summer.

"'In that small café,'" she sang, her voice thin and whispery, "'the park across the way . . .'"

Amid the island's little forest of leaning birches, their soft wood bent, as Marcia had explained, from the pounding they took in the hard Pocono winters, the two clung to each other with their unparalyzed arms, swaying together to the music on their unparalyzed legs, pressing together their unparalyzed trunks, and able now to hear the words only intermittently—". . . everything that's light and gay

. . . think of you . . . when night is new . . . seeing you"—before the song stopped. Someone across the lake had lifted the arm of the record player and switched it off, and the lights in the rec hall went out one at a time, and they could hear kids calling to one another, "Night! Good night!" Then the flashlights came on, and from the dance floor of the island ballroom, he and Marcia could see points of light flickering here and there as each of the kids— safe, healthy, unafraid, unharmed—traced a path back to the cabins.

"We have each other," Marcia whispered, removing his glasses and hungrily kissing his face. "No matter what happens in the world, we have each other's love. Bucky, I promise, you'll always have me singing to you and loving you and, whatever happens, I'll always be standing at your side."

"We do," he said to her, "we have each other's love." Yet what difference does that make, he thought, to Billy and Erwin and Ronnie? What difference does that make to their families? Hugging and kissing and dancing like lovesick teenagers ignorant of everything—what could that do for anyone?

*

WHEN HE GOT BACK to the cabin—everyone there in the deep sleep induced by a day full of hiking and swimming and playing ball—he found a note on his bed from Donald. "Call your grandmother," it said. Call her? But he'd spoken to her only a couple of hours earlier. He sped out the door and raced down to the phone booth wondering what had happened to her and thinking he should never have left her alone to come to camp. Of course she couldn't manage by herself, not when she had those pains in her chest every time she tried to carry anything up the stairs. He'd left her alone and now something had happened.

"Grandma, it's Eugene. What's wrong? Are you all right?"

"I'm all right. I have some news. That's why I called the camp. I didn't want to alarm you, but I thought you would want to know right away. It's not good news, Eugene. I wouldn't have called long distance otherwise. It's more tragedy. Mrs. Garonzik phoned from Elizabeth a few minutes ago. To speak to you."

"Jake," Bucky said.

"Yes," she said. "Jake is dead."

"How? How?"

"In action in France."

"I don't believe it. He was indestructible. He was a brick wall. He was six feet three inches tall and two hundred and fifteen pounds. He was a power-house. He can't be dead!"

"I'm afraid it's true, darling. His mother said he was killed in action. In a town whose name I can't remember now. I should have written it down. Eileen is there with the family."

The mention of Eileen shocked him anew. Jake had met Eileen McCurdy in high school, and she'd been Jake's girl throughout his years at Panzer. The two were to marry and set up house in Elizabeth as soon as he returned from the war.

"He was so big and with such good manners," his grandmother was saying. "Jake was one of the nicest boys you ever brought around. I can see him now, eating right in the kitchen here that first night he came home with you for dinner. Dave came too. Jake wanted 'Jewish food.' He ate sixteen latkes."

"He did. Yes, I remember. And we laughed, all of us laughed." Tears were coursing down Bucky's face now. "Dave's alive, though. Dave Jacobs is alive."

"I can't say that I know, darling. There's no way I would know. I assume so. I hope so. I haven't heard anything. But according to tonight's news, the war in France is not going well. They said on the radio that there are many dead. Terrible battles with the Germans. Many dead and many wounded."

"I can't lose both my friends," Bucky replied weakly, and when he hung up he headed not back to the cabin but down to the waterfront. There, despite the new rush of cold air pushing in, he sat on the diving dock and stared into the darkness, repeating to himself the lionizing epithets by which Jake was known on the sports page of the campus paper—Bruiser Jake, Big Jake, Man Mountain Jake . . . He could no more imagine Jake dead than he could imagine himself dead, which didn't serve, however, to stop his tears.

At about midnight, he walked back to the pier, but instead of going up the hill to the cabin, he turned and went out again along the wooden walkway to the diving dock. He proceeded to pace the length of the walkway until a dim light began to illuminate the lake, and he remembered that in just such a light another of the dearly beloved dead, his grandfather, would drink hot tea out of a glass—tea spiked in winter with a shot of schnapps—before heading off to buy his day's produce at the Mulberry Street market. When school was out Bucky sometimes went with him.

He was still struggling to bring himself under control so as to return to the cabin before anyone awoke, when the birds in the woods started singing. It was dawn at Camp Indian Hill. Soon there'd be the murmur of young voices from the cabins and then the happy shouting would begin.

ONCE A WEEK, Indian Night was celebrated separately in the boys' and girls' camps. At eight, all the boys came together at the campfire circle in a wide clearing high above the lake. At the center of the circle was a pit lined with flat stones. The logs there were stacked horizontally and laid crisscross in log-cabin style, tapering upward some three feet from the two large, heavy logs at the base. The fire logs were ringed by a stone barrier of small, picturesquely irregular boulders. Some eight or ten feet back from the stone barrier the circle of benches began. The seats were made of split logs and the bases of stone, and they extended concentrically outward until there were four rows in all, divided into three sections. The woods began some twenty feet back of the last row of benches. Mr. Blomback called the structure the Council Ring and the weekly gathering there the Grand Council.

At the edge of the Council Ring there was a teepee, larger and more elaborately embellished than the teepee at the camp entrance. That was the Council Tent, decorated at the top with bands of red, green, yellow, blue, and black, and with a border at the bottom of red and black. There was also a totem pole, whose crest was carved with the head of an eagle, and below that with a large unfurled wing jutting stiffly out to either side. The dominant colors of the totem pole were black, white, and red, the last two being the colors for the camp's color war. The totem pole stood about fifteen feet high and could be seen by anyone looking up from a boat on the lake. To the west, across the lake, where the girls were holding their own Indian Night, the sun was beginning to set, and full darkness would come by the time the Grand Council was over. Only faintly could you hear the post-dinner kitchen clatter from the dining lodge, while beyond the lake a striated sky drama, a long lava flow of burnt orange and bright pink and bloody crimson, registered the lingering end of the day. An iridescent, slow-moving summer twilight was creeping over Indian Hill, a splashy gift from the god of the horizon, if there was such a deity in the Indian pantheon.

The boys and their counselors—each designated a "brave" for the evening—arrived at Grand Council dressed in outfits that in large part came out of the crafts shop. All wore beaded headbands, fringed tunics that were originally ordinary shirts, and leggings that were trousers stitched with fringe at the outside seam. On their feet they wore moccasins, some cut from leather in the crafts shop and a good many of which were high-top sneakers that had been wrapped like moccasins at the ankle with bead and fringe. A number of the boys had feathers in their headbands—dropped bird plumage that they'd found in the woods—some wore beaded armbands tied inches above the elbow, and many carried canoe paddles that were painted with symbols colored, like the totem pole, in red, black, and white. Others had bows borrowed from the archery shack slung over their shoulders—bows without the arrows—and a few carried simulated tom-toms of tightly drawn calfskin and drum beaters with beaded handles that they made in crafts. Several held in their hands rattles that were decorated baking-powder cans filled with pebbles. The youngest campers used their own bed blankets wrapped around them as Indian robes, which also served to keep them warm as the evening temperature dropped.

Bucky's Indian outfit had been gathered together for him by the crafts counselor. Like the faces of the others, his had been darkened with cocoa powder to simulate an Indian's skin tone, and he had two diagonal stripes—"war paint"—applied to either cheek, one of black drawn with charcoal and the other of red drawn with lipstick. He sat next to Donald Kaplow and with the rest of the Comanche boys, who were seated farther down along the bench. Everywhere the boys loudly talked and joked until two campers carrying calfskin drums got up from the benches and walked to the stone surround of the campfire logs and, facing each other, began to solemnly bang on the drums while those carrying rattles shook them, no two in the same rhythm.

Then everyone turned to look toward the teepee. Mr. Blomback emerged from the oval doorway in a feather headdress, white feathers with brown tips all around his head and trailing behind in a tail down to below his waist. His tunic, his leggings, even his moccasins were elaborately decorated with leather fringe and bands of beadwork and long

tufts of what looked like human hair but was probably a woman's hairpiece from the five-and-ten. In
one hand he carried a club—"Great Chief Blomback's war club," Donald whispered—that was re-
plete with feathers, and in the other hand a peace
pipe, consisting of a long wooden stem ending in a
clay bowl and strung along the stem with still more
feathers.

All the campers stood until Mr. Blomback stol-
idly made his way from the teepee to the center of
the Council Ring. The drumming and the rattling
stopped, and the campers took their seats.

Mr. Blomback handed his war club and peace
pipe to the two drummers and, dramatically folding his arms over his chest, looked around at all the
campers on the encircling benches. His heavy appli-
cation of cocoa powder did not altogether cover his
prominent Adam's apple, but otherwise he looked
astonishingly like a real chief. In years gone by he
had saluted the braves Indian fashion—using an up-
raised right arm with the palm forward—and they
would collectively return the salute, simultaneously
grunting "Ugh!" But this greeting had to be abandoned with the arrival on the world scene of the

Nazis, who employed that salute to signify "Heil Hitler!"

"When first the brutal anthropoid stood up and walked erect," Mr. Blomback began, "—there was man! The great event was symbolized and marked by the lighting of the first campfire."

Donald turned to Bucky and whispered, "We get this every week. The little kids don't understand a word. No worse, I guess, than what happens in shul."

"For millions of years," Mr. Blomback continued, "our race has seen in this blessed fire the means and emblem of light, warmth, protection, friendly gathering, council."

He paused as the roar of an airplane engine passed over the camp. This happened now round the clock. An army air corps base had opened at the beginning of the war some seventy miles to the north, and Indian Hill was on its flyway.

"All the hallow of the ancient thoughts," Mr. Blomback said, "of hearth, fireside, home, is centered on its glow, and the home tie itself is weakened with the waning of the home fire. Only the ancient sacred fire of wood has power to touch and thrill the chords of primitive remembrance. Your campfire partner wins your love, and having camped in peace together—having marveled together at the morning sun, the evening light, the stars, the moon, the storms, the sunset, the dark of night—yours is a lasting bond of union, however wide your worlds may be apart."

Unfolding his two fringed arms, he extended them toward the assembly, and in unison the campers retorted to the stream of grandiloquence: "The campfire is the focal center of all primitive brotherhood. We shall not fail to use its magic."

The drummers now took up their tom-tom beat, and Donald whispered to Bucky, "An Indian historian. Somebody Seton. That's his god. Those are his words. Mr. Blomback uses the same Indian name as Seton: Black Wolf. He doesn't think any of this is nonsense."

Next a figure wearing the mask of a big-beaked bird stood in the front row and approached the ready-laid fire. He bowed his head to Mr. Blomback and then addressed the campers.

"Meetah Kola nayhoon-po omnicheeyay nee-chopi."

"It's our medicine man," whispered Donald. "It's Barry Feinberg."

"Hear me, my friends," the medicine man continued, translating his Indian sentence into English. "We are about to hold a council."

A boy stepped forward from the first row carrying several pieces of wood in his hand, one shaped like a bow, another a stick about a foot long with a sharpened end, and several smaller pieces. He set them on the ground near the medicine man.

"Now light we the council fire," the medicine man said, "after the manner of the forest children, not in the way of the white man, but—even as Wakonda himself doth light his fire—by the rubbing together of two trees in the storm, so cometh forth the sacred fire from the wood of the forest."

The medicine man knelt, and many of the campers stood to watch as he used the bow and the long, pointed drill and the other odd bits of wood to attempt to ignite a fire.

Donald whispered to Bucky, "This can take a while."

"Can it even be done?" Bucky whispered back.

"Chief Black Wolf can do it in thirty-one seconds. For the campers it's harder. They sometimes have to give in and do it in the way of the helpless white man, by striking a match."

Some of the campers were standing on their benches to get a better look. After a few minutes, Mr. Blomback sidled over to the medicine man and, gesturing as he spoke, quietly gave him some tips.

Everyone waited several minutes more before a whoop went up from the campers, as first there was smoke and then a spark, which when blown upon, ignited a small flame in the tinder of dry pine needles and birch bark shavings. The tinder in turn ignited the kindling at the base of the logs, and the campers chanted in unison, "Fire, fire, fire, burn! Flames, flames, flames, turn! Smoke, smoke, smoke, rise!"

Then, with the mournful loud-soft-soft-soft beat of the two tom-toms, the dancing began: the Mohawks did the snake dance, the Senecas the caribou dance, the Oneidas the dog dance, the Hopis the corn dance, the Sioux the grass dance. In one dance the braves jumped strenuously about with their heads high in the air, in another they did a skipping step on the balls of their feet with a double hop on each foot, in a third they carried deer antlers before them, made of crooked tree limbs bound together. Sometimes they howled like wolves and sometimes they yapped like dogs, and in the end, when it was fully dark and the burning fire alone lit the Council Ring, twenty of the campers, each armed with a war club and wearing necklaces of beads and claws, set out by the light of the fire to hunt Mishi-Mokwa, the Big Bear. Mishi-Mokwa was impersonated by the largest boy in camp, Jerome Hochberger, who slept across the aisle from Bucky. Jerome was wrapped in somebody's mother's old fur coat that he'd pulled up over his head.

"I am fearless Mishi-Mokwa," Jerome growled from within the coat. "I, the mighty mountain grizzly, king of all the western prairies."

The hunters had a leader who was also from Bucky's cabin, Shelly Schreiber. With the drums beating loudly behind him and light from the fire flashing on his painted face, Shelly said, "These are all my chosen warriors. We go hunting Mishi-Mokwa, he the Big Bear of the mountains, he that ravages our borders. We will surely seek and slay him."

Here a lot of the little kids began to call, "Slay him! Slay him! Slay Mishi-Mokwa!"

The hunters gave a war whoop, dancing as though they were bears on their hind legs. Then they set out looking for the trail of the Big Bear by conspicuously smelling the ground. When they reached him, he rose with a loud snarl, eliciting screams of fright from the small boys on the nearby benches.

"Ho, Mishi-Mokwa," said the leader of the hunters, "we have found you. If you do not come before I count to a hundred, I will brand you a coward wherever I go."

Suddenly, the bear sprang up at them, and as the campers cheered, the hunters proceeded to club him senseless with war clubs of straw wrapped in burlap. When he was stretched across the ground in the fur coat, the hunters danced around Mishi-Mokwa, each in turn grasping his lifeless paw and shouting, "How! How! How!" The campers' cheering continued, the delight enormous at finding themselves encompassed by murder and death.

Next, two counselors, a small one and a tall one, identified as Short Feather and Long Feather, told a series of animal tales that made the younger children scream with feigned horror, and then Mr. Blomback, having removed his feather headdress and set it down alongside his peace pipe and war club, led the boys in singing familiar camp songs for some twenty minutes, thus bringing them down to earth from the excitement of playing Indian. This was followed by his saying, "And here's the important war news from last week. Here's what's been happening beyond Indian Hill. In Italy, the British army broke across the Arno River into Florence. In the Pacific, United States assault forces invaded Guam, and Tojo—"

"Boo! Boo, Tojo!" a group of older boys called out.

"Tojo, the premier of Japan," Mr. Blomback resumed, "was ousted as chief of the Japanese army staff. In England, Prime Minister Churchill—"

"Yay, Churchill!"

"—predicted that the war against Germany could come to end earlier than expected. And right here in Chicago, Illinois, as many of you know by now, President Roosevelt was nominated for a fourth term by the Democratic National Convention."

Here a good half of the campers came to their feet, shouting, "Hurray! Hurray, President Roosevelt!" while somebody beat wildly on one of the tom-toms and somebody else shook a rattle.

"And now," said Mr. Blomback when it was quiet again, "bearing in mind the American troops fighting in Europe and the Pacific, and bearing in mind all of you boys who, like me, have relatives in the service, the next-to-last song to end the campfire will be 'God Bless America.' We dedicate it to all of those who are overseas tonight, fighting for our country."

After they had stood to sing "God Bless America," the boys raised their arms in their fringed sleeves, draped them around one another's shoulders, and, with one row of campers swaying in one direction and the rows of campers in front and behind swaying in the other, they sang "Till We Meet Again," the anthem of comradery that calmly brought to a close every Indian Night. When it was sung for the last Indian Night of the season, many of the home-bound campers would wind up in tears.

Meanwhile, Bucky alone had been brought to tears by the singing of "God Bless America" and the memory of the great college friend who had not been out of his thoughts since he'd learned of his death fighting in France. Bucky had done his best throughout the ceremonies to attend to what was going on around the fire as well as to listen to Donald quietly kibitzing beside him, but all he could really think about was Jake's death and Jake's life, about all that might have become of him had he lived. While the boys were hunting down the Big Bear, Bucky had been remembering the statewide college meet in the spring of '41 when Jake had set not just a Panzer College record but a U.S. collegiate record by throwing the shot fifty-six feet three inches. How did he do it, a reporter from the *Newark Star-Ledger* had asked him. Grinning widely— and flashing at Bucky his trophy with the tiny bronze shot-putter perched atop it, frozen at the point of the shot's release—Jake told him. "Easy," he said with a wink. "The left shoulder is high, the right shoulder is higher, the right elbow is even higher, and the right hand is the highest. There's the scheme. Follow that, and the shot takes care of itself." Easy. Everything for Jake was easy. He would surely have gone on to throw in the Olympics, would have gone on to marry Eileen as soon as he got home, would have garnered a job in college coaching . . . With all that talent, what could have stopped him?

Round the campfire
'Neath the stars so bright,
We have met in comradeship tonight.
Round about the whispering trees
Guard our golden memories.
And so, before we close our eyes in sleep
Let us pledge each other that we'll keep
Indian Hill's friendships deep,
Till we meet again.

After the singing of the farewell song, the campers buddied up in pairs and followed their counselors down from the benches around the dying campfire, which a couple of junior counselors stayed behind to extinguish. As they headed back to their cabins with their twinkling flashlights disappearing into the dark woods, an occasional war whoop went up from the departing boys, and some of the blanketed little ones, still under the spell of the blazing fire, could be heard gleefully shouting "How! How! How!" A few, by shining their flashlights upward from their chins while grimacing and widening their eyes, made monster faces to scare each other one last time before Indian Night was over. For close to an hour the voices of laughing and giggling children could be heard reverberating from cabin to cabin, and, even after everyone was asleep, the smell of wood smoke permeated the camp.

It was six untroubled days later—the best days at the camp so far, lavish July light thickly spread everywhere, six masterpiece mountain midsummer days, one replicating the other—that someone stumbled jerkily, as if his ankles were in chains, to the Comanche cabin's bathroom at three A.M. Bucky's bed was at the end of a row just the other side of the bathroom wall, and when he awakened he heard the person in there being sick. He reached under his bed for his glasses and looked down the aisle to see who it was. The empty bed was Donald's. He got up and, with his lips close to the bathroom door, quietly said, "It's Bucky. You need help?"

Donald replied weakly, "Something I ate. I'll be okay." But soon he was retching again, and Bucky, in his pajamas, waited on the edge of his bed for Donald to come out of the bathroom.

Gary Weisberg, whose bed was next to Bucky's, had awakened and, seeing Bucky sitting up, rose on his elbows and whispered, "What's the matter?"

"Donald. Upset stomach. Go back to sleep."

Donald finally emerged from the bathroom and

Bucky held his elbow with one hand and slipped an arm around his waist to help him back to bed. He got him under the covers and took his pulse.

"Normal," Bucky whispered. "How do you feel?"

Donald replied with his eyes shut. "Washed out. Chills."

When Bucky put his hand to Donald's forehead it felt warmer than it should. "You want me to take you to the infirmary? Fever and chills. Maybe you should see the nurse."

"I'll be okay," Donald said in a faint voice. "Just need sleep."

But in the morning, with Donald so feeble he couldn't get up from the bed to brush his teeth, Bucky again put his hand to the boy's forehead and said, "I'm taking you to the infirmary."

"It's the flu," Donald said. "Diving in the cold." He tried to smile. "Can't say I wasn't warned."

"Probably the cold did do it. But you're still running a temperature and you should be in the infirmary. Are you in pain? Does anything hurt?"

"My head."

"Severe?"

"Kind of."

The boys in the cabin had all gone off to breakfast without Donald and Bucky. Rather than waste time having Donald change into his clothes, Bucky slipped Donald's bathrobe over his pajamas in order to walk him in his slippers down to the small infirmary that stood close to the camp entrance. One of Indian Hill's two nurses would be on duty there.

"Let me help you up," Bucky said.

"I can do it," Donald said. But when he went to stand, he was unable to, and, startled, he fell backward onto the bed.

"My leg," he said.

"Which leg? Both legs?"

"My right leg. It's like it's dead."

"We're going to get you to the hospital."

"Why can't I walk?" Donald's voice was suddenly quavering with fear. "Why can't I use my leg?"

"I don't know," Bucky told him. "But the doctors will find out and get you back on your feet. You wait. Try to be calm. I'm calling an ambulance."

He ran as fast as he could down the hill to Mr. Blomback's office, thinking, Alan, Herbie, Ronnie, Jake—wasn't that enough? Now Donald too?

The camp director was in the dining lodge having breakfast with the campers and counselors. Bucky slowed to a walk as he entered the lodge and saw Mr. Blomback in his usual seat at the center table. It was one of the mornings especially loved by the campers, when the cook served pancakes and you could smell the rivers of maple syrup flooding the campers' plates. "Mr. Blomback," he said quietly, "can you step outside a moment? Something urgent."

Mr. Blomback got up and the two of them went out the door and walked a few steps from the dining lodge before Bucky said, "I think Donald Kaplow has polio. I left him in his bed. One leg is paralyzed. His head hurts him. He has a fever and he was up during the night being sick. We better call an ambulance."

"No, an ambulance will alarm everybody. I'll take him to the hospital in my car. You're sure it's polio?"

"His right leg is paralyzed," Bucky replied. "He can't stand on it. His head aches. He's completely done in. Doesn't that sound like polio?"

Bucky ran up the hill while Mr. Blomback got his car and drove after him and parked outside the cabin. Bucky wrapped Donald in a blanket, and he and Mr. Blomback helped him off the bed and out onto the porch that looked down to the lake, the two of them holding him up on either side. In the time Bucky had been gone, Donald's unparalyzed left leg had weakened, so his two feet dragged limply behind him as they carried him down the stairs and into the car.

"Don't speak to anyone yet," Mr. Blomback said to Bucky. "We don't want the kids to panic. We don't want the counselors to panic. I'm taking him to the hospital now. I'll call his family from there."

When Bucky looked at the boy lying in the back seat of the car with his eyes closed and beginning now to struggle to breathe, he remembered how on the second night at the lake Donald had done his dives even more confidently, with greater smoothness and balance, than he had on the first; he remembered how robust he'd been, how after Donald's finishing his repertoire, Bucky had worked with him for half an hour more on a swan dive. And he remembered how with each dive Donald had gotten better and better.

Bucky rapped on the window and Donald opened his eyes. "You're going to be all right," Bucky told him, and Mr. Blomback started away. Bucky ran alongside the car, calling in to Donald, "We're going to be diving again in a matter of days," even though the boy's deterioration was plainly discernible and the look in his eyes was gruesome—two feverish eyes scanning Bucky's face, frantically seeking a panacea that no one could provide.

Fortunately the campers were still at breakfast, and Bucky ran up the cabin steps to make up Donald's bed as best he could without the blanket in which he'd wrapped him. Then he went out onto the porch to look down at the lake, where his staff would be assembling in a little while, and to ask himself the obvious question: Who brought polio here if not me?

The boys in the cabin were told that Donald had been taken to the hospital with stomach flu and was to be kept there until he recovered. In fact, a spinal tap at the hospital confirmed that Donald Kaplow had polio, and his parents were notified by Mr. Blomback, and they set out from their home in Hazleton for Stroudsburg. Bucky put in his day at the waterfront, working with the counselors, spending time in the water with the young kids and at the diving board correcting the dives of the older kids, who were crazy about diving and who would do nothing else all day long if they were allowed. Then, when his workday was over and the

campers were back in their cabins, changing out
of their dirtied clothes for dinner, he took off his
glasses and went up on the high board and for half
an hour concentrated on doing every difficult dive
he knew. When he was finished and came out of
the water and put on his glasses, he still hadn't gotten what had happened out of his mind—the speed
with which it had happened or the idea that he had
made it happen. Or the idea that the outbreak of
polio at the Chancellor playground had originated
with him as well. All at once he heard a loud shriek.
It was the shriek of the woman downstairs from the
Michaels family, terrified that her child would catch
polio and die. Only he didn't just hear the shriek—
he was the shriek.

THEY TOOK THE CANOE to the island again that
night. Marcia as yet knew nothing about Donald
Kaplow's illness. Mr. Blomback intended to notify
the entire camp at breakfast the following morning,
in the company of Dr. Huntley, the camp physician from Stroudsburg, who visited the camp regularly and, along with the camp nurses, was usually
called upon to treat little more than ringworm, im-
petigo, pinkeye, ivy poisoning, and, at worst, a bro-

ken bone. Though Mr. Blomback expected there would be some parents who would immediately remove their children from the camp, he was hoping that with Dr. Huntley's help in minimizing fear and curtailing any panic, he could carry on operating normally to the end of the season. He had confided this to Bucky when he returned from the hospital and reminded him to say nothing and to leave the announcement to him. Donald's condition had worsened. He now had excruciating muscle and joint pain and would probably need an iron lung to help him breathe. His parents had arrived, but by then Donald had been placed in isolation, and because of the danger of contagion, they hadn't been allowed to see him. The doctors had commented to Mr. Blomback on the rapidity with which Donald's flu-like symptoms had evolved into the most life-threatening strain of the disease.

All of this Bucky recounted to Marcia once they reached the island.

She gasped at his words. She was seated on the blanket and put her face in her hands. Bucky was pacing around the clearing, unable as yet to tell her the rest. It had been hard enough for her to hear about Donald without her having to hear in the next breath about him.

"I have to talk to my father" were the first words she spoke. "I have to phone him."

"Why not let Mr. Blomback tell the camp first?"

"He should have told the camp already. You cannot wait around with a thing like this."

"You think he should disband the camp?"

"That's what I want to ask my father. This is terrible. What about the rest of the boys in your cabin?"

"They seem to be all right so far."

"What about you?" she asked.

"I feel fine," he said. "I have to tell you, I spent two sessions at the lake with Donald a few days back. I was helping him with his dives. He couldn't have been healthier."

"When was that?"

"About a week ago. After dinner. I let him dive in the cold. That was probably an error. A bad error."

"Oh, Bucky, this isn't your fault. It's just so frightening. I'm frightened for you. I'm frightened for my sisters. I'm frightened for every kid in the camp.

I'm frightened for myself. One case isn't one case in a summer camp full of kids living side by side. It's like a lit match in the dry woods. One case here is a hundred times more dangerous than it is in a city."

She remained seated and he resumed pacing. He was afraid to approach her because he was afraid to infect her, if he hadn't infected her already. If he hadn't infected everyone! The little ones at the lake! His waterfront staff! The twins, whom he kissed every night at the dining lodge! When, in his agitation, he removed his glasses to rub nervously at his eyes, the birch trees encircling them looked in the moonlight like a myriad of deformed silhouettes—their lovers' island haunted suddenly with the ghosts of polio victims.

"We have to go back," Marcia said. "I have to phone my father."

"I told Mr. Blomback I wouldn't tell anyone."

"I don't care. I am responsible for my sisters, if nothing else. I have to tell my father what has happened and ask him what to do. I'm scared, Bucky. I'm very scared. It was always as if polio would never notice that there were kids in these woods—that it couldn't find them here. I thought if they just stayed in camp and didn't go anywhere they'd be okay. How could it possibly hunt them down *here?*"

He couldn't tell her. She was too aghast to be told. And he was too confused by the magnitude of it all to do the telling. The magnitude of what had been done. The magnitude of what *he* had done.

Marcia got up from the blanket and folded it, and they pulled the canoe into the water and started back to camp. It was close to ten when they got to the landing. The counselors were up in the cabins getting their campers into bed. The lights were on in Mr. Blomback's office, but otherwise the camp seemed deserted. There was no line waiting to use the pay phone, though there'd be one tomorrow, once word was out about Donald and the turn that camp life had taken.

Marcia closed the folding door of the phone booth so there was no chance of her being overheard by anyone who might be about, and Bucky stood beside the booth, trying to tell from her reactions what Dr. Steinberg was saying. Marcia's voice was muffled, so all Bucky heard standing outside the booth were the insects droning and humming, sending his mind back to that chokingly close eve-

ning in Newark when he had sat out on the rear
porch with Dr. Steinberg, eating that wonderful
peach.

Her distress seemed to lessen once she heard her
father's voice at the other end of the phone, and
after only a few minutes she lowered herself onto
the booth's little seat and talked to him from there.
Bucky was supposed to have gone into Stroudsburg
with Carl at noon that day to buy her engagement
ring. Now the engagement was forgotten. It was
polio only that was on Marcia's mind, as it had been
on his all summer. There was no escape from polio,
and not because it had followed him to the Poconos
but because he had carried it to the Poconos with
him. How, Marcia asked, had polio hunted us down
here? Through the contagion of the newcomer, her
boyfriend! Remembering all the boys who'd gotten polio while he was working earlier in the summer at Chancellor, remembering the scene that had
erupted on the field the afternoon Kenny Blumenfeld had to be restrained from assaulting Horace,
Bucky thought that it wasn't the moron that Kenny
should have wanted to kill for spreading polio—it
was the playground director.

Marcia opened the door and stepped out of the

booth. Whatever her father told her had calmed her down, and with her arms around Bucky, she said, "I got so frightened for my sisters. I know you'll be all right, you're strong and fit, but I got so worried for those two girls."

"What did your father say?" he asked, speaking with his head turned so that he was not breathing into her face.

"He said that he's going to call Bill Blomback but that it sounds as if he's doing everything there is to do. He says you don't evacuate two hundred and fifty kids because of one case of polio. He says the kids should go on with their regular activities. He says he thinks a lot of parents are going to panic and pull their kids out. But that I shouldn't panic or panic the girls. He asked about you. I said you've been a rock. Oh, Bucky, I feel better. He and my mother are going to drive up this weekend instead of going down the shore. They want to reassure the girls themselves."

"Good," he said, and though he held her tightly, he was mindful to kiss her hair and not her lips when they separated for the night, as if by this time that could alter anything.

*

THE NEXT MORNING, at the close of breakfast, Mr. Blomback swung the cowbell whose ringing always preceded his announcements to the camp. The campers quieted down as he rose to his feet. "Good morning, boys and girls. I have a serious message to deliver to you this morning," he said, speaking evenly, with nothing in his voice to indicate alarm. "It concerns the health of one of our counselors. He is Donald Kaplow of the Comanche cabin. Donald became ill here two nights ago and yesterday morning awakened with a high fever. Mr. Cantor quickly notified me of Donald's condition, and it was decided that he should be taken to Stroudsburg Hospital. There, tests were performed and it was determined that Donald has contracted polio. His parents have arrived at the hospital to be with him. He is being treated and cared for by the hospital staff. I have Dr. Huntley, the camp physician, here with me, and he wants to say a few words to you."

The counselors and campers were, of course, startled to learn that everything in camp had suddenly changed—that everything in *life* had changed—and they waited in silence to hear what the doctor had to tell them. He was a middle-aged man with an unruffled manner who had been the camp's physician since its inception. He had a bland, reassuring way about him that was enhanced by his rimless spectacles and his thinning white hair and his pale plain face. He was dressed like no one else in camp, in a suit, white shirt, tie, and dark shoes.

"Good morning. For those of you who don't already know me, I'm Dr. Huntley. I know that if and when any of you ever feel ill, you tell your counselor and your counselor arranges for you to see Miss Rudko or Miss Southworth, the camp nurses, and if necessary, you see me. Well, I want to encourage you to continue with this same procedure during the days and weeks ahead. Any sign of illness, promptly notify your counselor, as you always would. If you have a sore throat, if you have a stiff neck, if you have an upset stomach, notify your counselor. If you have a headache, if you think you have a fever, notify your counselor. If you don't feel well generally, notify your counselor. Your counselor will get you to the nurse, who will look after you and who will be in touch with me. Because I want you all to be well so as to enjoy the remaining weeks of the summer."

Having spoken no more than those few calming

words, Dr. Huntley sat down and Mr. Blomback stood again. "I want all you campers to know that before the morning is over I am going to phone each of your families to tell them about this development. In the meantime, I'd like to see the head counselors in my office right after breakfast. Everyone else," he said, "that's it for now. Today's program is unchanged. Regular activities. Go out into the sunshine and have a good time—it's another beautiful day."

Marcia rushed off to Mr. Blomback's office with the three other head counselors, and Bucky, instead of going down to the waterfront, which he'd had every intention of doing upon leaving the dining lodge, found himself running to catch up to Dr. Huntley before he stepped into his car, parked by the flagpole, and drove back to town.

Behind him he heard his named called. "Bucky! Wait a minute! Wait for us!" It was the Steinberg twins, racing to catch him. "Wait up!"

"Girls, I have to see Dr. Huntley."

"Bucky," said one of the twins, grabbing his hand, "what are we supposed to *do?*"

"You heard Mr. Blomback. Just go on with your activities."

"But polio—!" When they tried to reach out to hold him around the waist and nuzzle for reassurance against his broad chest, he instantly backed away for fear of breathing into the two identical panic-stricken faces.

"Don't you worry about polio," he said. "There's nothing to worry about. Sheila, Phyllis, I have to run—it's very important," and he left them there unconsoled, cringing up against each other.

"But we need you!" one of them called after him. "Marcia's with Mr. Blomback!"

"This afternoon!" he called back. "I promise! I'll see you soon!"

Dr. Huntley had opened the door to his car and was just getting in when Bucky reached him. "Dr. Huntley, I have to talk to you. I'm the waterfront director in the boys' camp. Bucky Cantor."

"Yes, Bill Blomback mentioned you."

"Dr. Huntley, I have to tell you something. I came up from Newark a week ago Friday. I'd been working there in a playground in the Weequahic neighborhood, where there's an epidemic of polio. Donald Kaplow and I were working out at the waterfront together after dinner for two nights. We've had lunch side by side every day. We pass each other in the cabin. I sat next to him at Indian Night. Now he's come down with polio. Doctor, am I the one who gave it to him? Am I going to give it to others? Is that possible?"

By now Dr. Huntley had stepped out of the car, the better to catch the overwrought words being spoken to him by this perfectly vigorous-looking young man. "How do you feel?" he asked Bucky.

"I feel fine."

"Well, the chances are slight that you are a healthy infected carrier. Though it could happen, it would be a very uncommon abnormality. Most usually, the carrier stage coincides with the clinical stage. But to ease your mind," the doctor said, "to be a hundred percent sure, we should take you in for a spinal tap and draw off some spinal fluid for analysis. Certain changes to spinal fluid are indicative of polio. We should do that right away, this morning, to put your mind at rest. You can drive with me to the hospital, and then we'll call Carl to drive you back here."

Bucky raced down to the waterfront to tell the staff he'd be gone for the morning and to put one of the senior counselors in charge till he returned, and then he met Dr. Huntley, who was waiting for

him in his car for the ride into Stroudsburg. If only
the test revealed that he was not the person responsible! If only he were about to be proved blameless!
Then, when the examination at the hospital was
over and everything certified to be okay, he could
stop off at the Stroudsburg jewelry store on the way
back to camp to buy the engagement ring for Marcia. He hoped to be able to afford something set
with a genuine jewel.

Later that day, the cars began to arrive to take
campers home. They continued arriving into the
late evening and on into the next day, so that within
forty-eight hours after Mr. Blomback had announced to the camp at breakfast that one of the
counselors had come down with polio, more than
a hundred of the two hundred and fifty campers
had been removed by their parents. The next day,
two more boys in Bucky's cabin—one of them Jerome Hochberger, the big boy in the fur coat who
had played the bear on Indian Night—were diagnosed with polio and the entire camp was immediately shut down. Another nine of the Indian Hill
campers fell ill and had to be hospitalized with polio when they got home, among them Marcia's sister Sheila.

3

Reunion

We never saw Mr. Cantor in the neighborhood again. The result of the spinal tap administered at Stroudsburg Hospital came back positive, and though he displayed no symptoms for almost forty-eight hours more, he was rushed onto the contagion ward, where he could have no visitors. And finally the cataclysm began—the monstrous headache, the enfeebling exhaustion, the severe nausea, the raging fever, the unbearable muscle ache, followed in another forty-eight hours by the paralysis. He was there for three weeks before he no longer needed catheterization and enemas, and they moved him upstairs and began treatment with steamed woolen hot packs wrapped around his arms and legs, all of which were initially stricken. He underwent four torturous sessions of the hot packs a day, together lasting as long as four to six hours. Fortunately his respiratory muscles hadn't been affected, so he never had to be moved inside an iron lung to assist with his breathing, a prospect that he dreaded more than any other. And his learning that Donald Kaplow was still in the same hospital, barely being kept alive in an iron lung, filled him with terror and tears. Donald the diver, Donald the discus thrower, Donald the naval-air-pilot-to-be, no longer powered by his lungs and his limbs!

Eventually Mr. Cantor was moved by ambulance to a Sister Kenny Institute in Philadelphia, where, by this point in the summer, the epidemic was nearly as bad as it was in Newark and the hospital's wards were so crowded that he was fortunate to get a bed. There the hot pack treatment continued, along with painful stretching of the contracted muscles of his arms and legs and of his back—which the paralysis had twisted—in order to "reeducate" them. He spent the next fourteen months in rehabilitation at the Kenny Institute, gradually recovering the full use of his right arm and partial use of his legs, though he was left with a twisted lower spine that had to be corrected several years later by a surgical fusion and a bone graft and the insertion of metal rods attached to the spine. The recuperation from the surgery put him on his back in a body cast for six months, tended day and night by his grandmother. He was at the Kenny Institute when President Roosevelt unexpectedly died, in April 1945, and the country went into mourning. He was there when defeated Germany surrendered in May, when the atomic bombs were dropped on Hiroshima and Nagasaki in August, and when Japan asked to surrender to the Allies a few days later. World War II was over, his buddy Dave would be coming home unscathed from fighting in Europe, America was jubilant, and he was still in the hospital, disfigured and maimed.

At the Kenny Institute he was one of the few who weren't bedridden. After a few weeks, he got into a wheelchair and was using it when he returned to Newark. There he continued treatment as an outpatient and, in time, recovered all the muscle function in his right leg. His bills had been astronomical, thousands and thousands of dollars, but they were paid by the Sister Kenny Institute and the March of Dimes.

He never returned to teaching phys ed at Chancellor or supervising the playground, nor did he

realize his dream of coaching track and field at
Weequahic. He left education entirely, and after
a couple of unfortunate starts—employed first as
a clerk in the Avon Avenue grocery store that had
once been his grandfather's and then, when as a result of his disability he could find no other job, as
a service station attendant on Springfield Avenue,
where he was utterly unlike the crude guys working
there and where customers sometimes called him
Gimp—he took the civil service exam. Because he
scored high and was a college graduate, he found a
desk job with the post office downtown and so was
able to support himself and his grandmother on his
government salary.

I ran into him in 1971, years after I had graduated from architecture school and had set up my office in a building diagonally across the street from
the main Newark post office. We could have passed
each other on Broad Street a hundred times before
the day I finally recognized him.

I was one of the Chancellor Avenue playground
boys who, in the summer of '44, contracted polio
and was then confined to a wheelchair for a year
before protracted rehabilitation made it possible
for me to locomote myself on a crutch and a cane,

and with my two legs braced, as I do to this day. Some ten years back, after serving an apprenticeship with an architectural firm in the city, I started a company with a mechanical engineer who, like me, had had polio as a kid. We opened a consulting and contracting firm specializing in architectural modification for wheelchair accessibility, our options ranging from building additional rooms onto existing houses down to installing grab bars, lowering closet rods, and relocating light switches. We design and install ramps and wheelchair lifts, we widen doorways, we make bathroom, bedroom, and kitchen modifications—everything to improve life for wheelchair-bound people like my partner. The wheelchair-bound may require household structural changes that can be costly, but we do our best to keep to our estimates and to hold prices down. Along with the quality of our work, this is what largely accounts for our success. The rest was the luck of location and timing, of being the only such outfit in populous northern New Jersey at a moment when serious attention was beginning to be paid to the singular needs of the disabled.

Sometimes you're lucky and sometimes you're not. Any biography is chance, and, beginning at

conception, chance—the tyranny of contingency—
is everything. Chance is what I believed Mr. Cantor
meant when he was decrying what he called God.

Mr. Cantor still had a withered left arm and useless left hand, and the damage to the muscles in his
left calf caused a dip in his gait. The leg had begun
getting much weaker in recent years, both the lower
and the upper leg, and the limb had also begun to
be severely painful for the first time since his rehabilitation nearly thirty years before. As a result, following a doctor's examination and a couple of visits
to his hospital's brace shop, he had taken to wearing
a full leg brace beneath his trousers to support his
left leg. It didn't ease the pain much, but along with
a cane it helped with balance and steadiness on his
feet. However, if things continued to deteriorate—
as they often do in later years for many polio survi-
vors who come to suffer what is known as post-po-
lio syndrome—it might not be long, he said, before
he wound up back in a chair.

We came upon each other at noon one spring
day in 1971 on busy Broad Street, midway between
where the two of us worked. It was I who spotted
him, even though he wore a protective mustache
now and, at the age of fifty, his once black hair was

no longer cut in a military crewcut but rose atop his head like a white thicket—the mustache was white as well. And he no longer, of course, had that athletic, pigeon-toed stride. The sharp planes of his face were padded by the weight he'd gained, so he was nowhere as striking as when the head beneath the tawny skin looked to be machined to the most rigorous rectilinear specifications—when it was a young man's head unabashedly asserting itself. That original face was now interred in another, fleshier face, a concealment people often see when looking with resignation at their aging selves in the mirror. No trace of the compact muscleman remained, the muscles having melted away while the compactness had burgeoned. Now he was simply stout.

I was by then thirty-nine, a short, heavy man myself, bearded and bearing little if any resemblance to the frail kid I'd been growing up. When I realized on the street who he was, I got so excited I shouted after him, "Mr. Cantor! Mr. Cantor! It's Arnold Mesnikoff. From the Chancellor playground. Alan Michaels was my closest friend. He sat next to me all through school." Though I'd never forgotten Alan, I hadn't uttered his name aloud in the many years since he'd died, back in that decade when it seemed that the greatest menaces on earth were war, the atomic bomb, and polio.

After our first emotional street meeting, we began to eat lunch together once a week in a nearby diner, and that's how I got to hear his story. I turned out to be the first person to whom he'd ever told the whole of the story, from beginning to end, and—as he came to confide more intimately with each passing week—without leaving very much out. I tried my best to listen closely and to take it all in while he found the words for everything that had been on his mind for the better part of his life. Talking like this seemed to him to be neither pleasant nor unpleasant—it was a pouring forth that before long he could not control, neither an unburdening nor a remedy so much as an exile's painful visit to the irreclaimable homeland, the beloved birthplace that was the site of his undoing. We two had not been especially close on the playground—I was a poor athlete, a shy, quiet boy, delicately built. But the fact that I had been one of the kids hanging around Chancellor that horrible summer—that I was the best friend of his playground favorite and, like Alan and like him, had come down with polio—made him bluntly candid in a self-searing manner that sometimes astonished me, the auditor whom he'd never before known as an adult, the auditor now inspiring his confidence the way, as kids, I and the others had been inspired by him.

By and large he had the aura of ineradicable failure about him as he spoke of all that he'd been silent about for years, not just crippled physically by polio but no less demoralized by persistent shame. He was the very antithesis of the country's greatest prototype of the polio victim, FDR, disease having led Bucky not to triumph but to defeat. The paralysis and everything that came in its wake had irreparably damaged his assurance as a virile man, and he had withdrawn completely from that whole side of life. Mostly Bucky considered himself a gender blank—as in a cartridge that is blank—an abashing self-assessment for a boy who'd come of age in an era of national suffering and strife when men were meant to be undaunted defenders of home and country. When I told him that I had a wife and two children, he replied that he never had it in him to date anyone, let alone to marry, after he was paralyzed. He could never show his withered arm and withered leg to anyone other than a doctor or, when she was living, his grandmother. It was she who had devotedly taken care of him when he left the Kenny Institute, she who, despite her chest pains having been diagnosed as serious heart trouble, had boarded the train from Newark to visit him in Philadelphia every Sunday afternoon, without fail, for the fourteen months he was there.

She was now long dead, but until he found himself in the middle of the 1967 Newark riots—during which a house down the street had burned to the ground and shots had been fired from a nearby rooftop—he'd lived on in their small walkup flat in the tenement on Barclay near Avon. He had the flights of outside stairs to navigate—stairs that he'd once liked to take three at a time—and so, whatever the season, however icy or slippery they were, he laboriously climbed them so as to stay on in the third-floor flat where his grandmother's love had once been limitless and where the mothering voice that had never been unkind could be best remembered. Even though, *especially* though, no loved one from the past remained in his life, he could—and often did, involuntarily, while mounting the steps to his door at the end of the workday—summon up a clear picture of his kneeling grandmother, scrubbing their flight of stairs once a week with a stiff brush and a pail of sudsy water or cooking for their little family over the coal stove. That's the most he could do for his emotional reliance on women.

And never, never since he'd left for Camp Indian Hill in July 1944, had he returned to Weequahic or paid a visit to the gym where he'd taught at the Chancellor Avenue School or to the Chancellor playground.

"Why not?" I asked.

"Why would I? I was the Typhoid Mary of the Chancellor playground. I was the playground polio carrier. I was the Indian Hill polio carrier."

His idea of himself in this role hit me hard. Nothing could have prepared me for its severity.

"Were you? There's certainly no proof that you were."

"There's no proof that I wasn't," he said, speaking, as he mostly did during our lunchtime conversations, either looking away from my face to some unseen point in the distance or looking down into the food on our plates. He did not seem to want me, or perhaps anyone, staring inquisitively into his eyes.

"But you got polio," I told him. "You got it like

the rest of us unfortunate enough to get polio eleven years too soon for the vaccine. Twentieth-century medicine made its phenomenal progress just a little too slowly for us. Today childhood summers are as sublimely worry-free as they should be. The significance of polio has disappeared completely. Nobody anymore is defenseless like we were. But to speak specifically about you, the chances are you caught polio from Donald Kaplow rather than that you gave it to him."

"And what about Sheila, the Steinberg twin— who'd she get it from? Look, it's far too late in the day to be rehashing all that now," he said, oddly, having rehashed nearly everything with me already. "Whatever was done, was done," he said. "Whatever I did, I did. What I don't have, I live without."

"But even if it were possible that you were a carrier, you would have been an unsuspecting carrier. Surely you haven't lived all these years punishing yourself, despising yourself, for something you didn't do. That's much too harsh a sentence."

There was a pause, during which he studied that spot that engaged him—to the side of my head and somewhere in the far distance, that spot which more than likely was 1944.

"What I've lived with mostly all these years," he said, "is Marcia Steinberg, if you want the truth. I cut myself free of many things, but I was never able to do that with her. All these years later, and there are times that I still think I recognize her on the street."

"As she was at twenty-two?"

He nodded, and then, to round out the disclosure, he said, "On Sundays I surely don't want to be thinking about her, yet that's when I mostly do. And nothing comes of my trying not to."

Some people are forgotten the moment you turn your back on them; that was not the case for Bucky with Marcia. Marcia's memory had endured.

He reached into his jacket pocket with his unwithered hand and took out an envelope and presented it to me. It was addressed to Eugene Cantor at 17 Barclay Street and postmarked at Stroudsburg, July 2, 1944.

"Go ahead," he said. "I brought it so you can look at it. I got it when she'd been away at camp just a few days."

The note I took from the envelope was written

in perfect Palmer Method cursive on a small sheet
of pale green stationery. It read:

My man my man my man my man my man
my man my man my man my man my man
my man my man my man my man my man
my man my man my man my man my man

All the way to the bottom of the page and halfway
down the other side, the two words were repeated
over and over, all of them evenly supported on an
invisible straight line. The letter was signed with
just her initial, *M*, a tall, beautifully formed capital
exhibiting a little flourish in the loop and the stem,
followed by "(as in My Man)."

I placed the single page back in the envelope and
returned it to him.

"A twenty-two-year-old writes to her first lover.
You must have been pleased to get such a letter."

"I got it when I came home from work. I kept
it in my pocket during dinner. I took it with me
to bed. I went to sleep with it in my hand. Then
I was awakened by the phone. My grandmother
slept across the hall. She was alarmed. 'Who can
it be at this hour?' I went into the kitchen to answer. It was a few minutes after midnight by the

clock there. Marcia was calling from the phone booth behind Mr. Blomback's office. She'd been in bed in her cabin, unable to sleep, so she got up and dressed and came out in the dark to call me. She wanted to know if I had received the letter. I said I had. I said I was her man two hundred and eighteen times over—she could depend on that. I said that I was her man forever. Then she told me that she wanted to sing to her man to put him to sleep. I was at the kitchen table in my skivvies in the dark and sweating like a pig from the heat. It had been another whopper of a day, and it hadn't cooled off any by midnight. The lights were out in all the flats across the way. I don't think anyone was awake on our whole street."

"Did she sing to you?"

"A lullaby. It wasn't one I knew, but it was a lullaby. She sang it very, very softly. There it was, all by itself, over the phone. Probably one she remembered from when she was a kid."

"So you had a weakness for her soft voice too."

"I was stunned. Stunned by so much happiness. I was so stunned that I whispered into the phone, 'Are you really as wonderful as this?' I couldn't believe such a girl existed. I was the luckiest guy in the world. And unstoppable. You understand me? With all that love of hers, how could I ever be stopped?"

"Then you lost her," I said. "How did you lose her? That you haven't told me yet."

"No, I haven't. I wouldn't let Marcia see me. That's how it happened. Look, maybe I've said enough." Suddenly, made uneasy by a pang of shame for the sentiments he'd just confided, he flushed deeply. "What the hell got me started? That letter. Finding that letter. I should never have gone looking for it."

With his elbow on the table he dropped his reddened face into his good hand and with his fingertips rubbed at his closed eyelid. We had reached the hardest part of the story.

"What happened to end it with Marcia?" I asked.

"When she came up to Stroudsburg to the hospital, when I was out of isolation, I had them turn her away. She left me a note telling me that her kid sister had only a mild, nonparalytic case and after three weeks recovered completely. I was relieved to learn that, but I still didn't want to resume my relations with the family. Marcia tried a second time to see me when I was transferred down to Philadelphia. That time I let her. We had a terrible argument. I didn't know she had it in her—I'd never seen her openly angry at anyone before. After that, she never came back. We never made contact again. Her father tried to talk to me when I was in Philadelphia, but I wouldn't take the call. When I was working at the Esso station on Springfield Avenue, out of the blue one day he pulled in for gas. That was a long way for him to go for gas."

"Was he there for her? To try to get you to come back?"

"I don't know. Maybe. I let another guy take the pump. I hid. I knew I was no match for Dr. Steinberg. I have no idea what happened to his daughter. I don't want to know. Whoever she married, let them and their children be happy and enjoy good health. Let's hope their merciful God will have blessed them with all that before He sticks His shiv in their back."

It was an arrestingly harsh utterance from the likes of Bucky Cantor, and, momentarily, he seemed to have perturbed himself by making it.

"I owed her her freedom," he finally said, "and I gave it to her. I didn't want the girl to feel stuck with me. I didn't want to ruin her life. She hadn't fallen in love with a cripple, and she shouldn't be stuck with one."

"Wasn't that up to her to decide?" I asked. "A damaged man is sometimes very attractive to a certain type of woman. I know from experience."

"Look, Marcia was a sweet, naive, well-brought-up girl with kindly, responsible parents who had taught her and her sisters to be polite and obliging," Bucky said. "She was a young new first-grade teacher, wet behind the ears. A slight slip of a thing, inches shorter even than me. It didn't help her being more intelligent than me—she still didn't have any idea of how to go about getting out of her mess. So I did it for her. I did what had to be done."

"You've given this a lot of thought," I said. "All your thought, it sounds like."

He smiled for one of the few times during our talks, a smile very like a frown, denoting weariness more than good cheer. There was no lightness in him. That was missing, as were the energy and the industry that were once at the center of him. And, of course, the athletic ingredient had completely vanished. It wasn't only an arm and a leg that were useless. His original personality, all that vital purposefulness that would hit you in the face the moment you met him, seemed itself to have been stripped away, lifted from him in shreds as though it were the thin swatch of bark that he'd peeled from the birch tree the first night with Marcia on the island in the lake at Indian Hill. We had been together one day a week at lunch over a period of a few months and never once did he lighten up, not even when he said, "That song she liked, 'I'll Be Seeing You'—I've never been able to forget that either. Soupy, sappy, yet it looks like I'll remember it for as long as I live. I don't know what would happen if I had to hear it again."

"You'd bawl."

"I might."

"You'd have a right," I said. "Anyone would be miserable, having renounced a true mate like that."

"Oh, my old playground buddy," he said, with more feeling than he'd spoken yet, "I never thought that's how it would end with her. Never."

"When she got angry with you—the time she came to see you in Philadelphia—"

"I never saw her again after that."

"You've said. But what happened?"

He was in a wheelchair, he told me, a glori-

ous autumn Saturday in mid-October, still warm
enough for them to go outdoors and for her to
sit on a bench on the lawn in front of the Sister
Kenny Institute, beneath the branches of a tree
whose leaves had turned and begun to fall, but not
so warm that the polio epidemic in the northeastern states hadn't finally dissipated and died away.
By then Bucky had not seen her or spoken to her in
nearly three months, so she hadn't yet had a chance
to observe how crippled he was. There had been
an exchange of correspondence, not between Bucky
and Marcia but between Bucky and Marcia's father.
Dr. Steinberg had written to tell Bucky that he had
an obligation to allow Marcia to visit him and tell
him directly what was on her mind. "Marcia and
the family," wrote Dr. Steinberg, "deserve better
from you than this." Against a handwritten letter
on personalized hospital stationery from a man of
the doctor's stature, Bucky, of course, had no de-
fense, and so the date and time of Marcia's visit
were set, and the quarrel began almost immediately
upon her arrival, when he noticed right off that her
hair had grown out since he'd seen her last, making
her look more womanly than she had at camp and
prettier now than ever. She had dressed with gloves

and a hat, just like the proper teacher whom he'd first fallen for.

There was nothing she could say that would change his mind, he announced, however much he would have loved just to reach out with his good hand and touch her face. Instead, he used his good hand to grasp his dead arm around the wrist and raise it to the level of her eyes. "Look," he said. "This is what I look like."

She did not speak, but she did not blink either. No, he told her, he was no longer man enough to be a husband and a father, and it was irresponsible of her to think otherwise.

"Irresponsible of *me?*" she cried.

"To be the noble heroine. Yes."

"What are you talking about? I'm not trying to be anything other than the person who loves you and wants to marry you and be your wife." And then she advanced the gambit that she had no doubt rehearsed on the train down. "Bucky, it's not complicated, really," she told him. "*I'm* not complicated. Remember me? Remember what I said to you the night before I left for camp in June? 'We'll do it perfectly.' Well, we will. Nothing has changed that. I'm just an ordinary girl who wants to be happy.

You make me happy. You always have. Why won't
you now?"

"Because it's no longer the night before you left
for camp. Because I'm no longer the person you fell
in love with. You delude yourself if you think that
I am. You're only doing what your conscience tells
you is right—I understand that."

"You don't at all! You're speaking nonsense! It's
you who's trying to be noble by refusing to talk to
me and refusing to see me. By telling me to leave
you alone. Oh, Bucky, you're being so blind!"

"Marcia, marry a man who isn't maimed, who's
strong, who's fit, who's got all that a prospective father needs. You could have anyone, a lawyer, a doctor—someone as smart as you are and as educated
as you are. *That's* what you and your family deserve.
And that's what you should have."

"You are infuriating me so by talking like this!
Nothing in my entire life has ever infuriated me as
much as what you are doing right now! I have never
known anyone other than you who finds such comfort in castigating himself!"

"That's not what I'm doing. That's an absolute
distortion of what I'm doing. I just happen to see
the implications of what's happened and you don't.

You won't. Listen to me: things aren't the way they were before the summer. Look at me. Things couldn't be more different. Look."

"Stop this, please. I've seen your arm and *I don't care.*"

"Then look at my leg," he said, pulling up his pajama bottoms.

"Stop, I beg you! You think it's your body that's deformed, but what's truly deformed is your mind!"

"Another good reason to save yourself from me. Most women would be delighted if a cripple volunteered to get out of their life."

"Then I'm not most women! And you're not just a cripple! Bucky, you've *always* been this way. You could never put things at the right distance— never! You're always holding yourself accountable when you're *not.* Either it's terrible God who is accountable, or it's terrible Bucky Cantor who is accountable, when in fact, accountability belongs to *neither.* Your attitude toward God—it's juvenile, it's just plain silly."

"Look, your God is not to my liking, so don't bring Him into the picture. He's too mean for me. He spends too much time killing children."

"And that is nonsense too! Just because you got polio doesn't give you the right to say ridiculous things. You have no idea what God is! No one does or can! You are being asinine—and you're not asinine. You sound so ignorant—and you're not ignorant. You are being crazy—and you're not crazy. You were never crazy. You were perfectly sane. Sane and sound and strong and smart. But this! Spurning my love for you, spurning my family—I refuse to be a party to such insanity!"

Here the obstinate resistance collapsed, and she threw her hands up over her face and began to sob. Other patients who were entertaining visitors on nearby benches or being pushed in wheelchairs along the paved path in front of the institute could not but notice the petite, pretty, well-dressed young woman, seated beside a patient in a wheelchair, who was so visibly swept away by her sorrow.

"I'm completely baffled by you," she told him through her tears. "If only you could have gone into the war, you might—oh, I don't know what you might. You might have been a soldier and gotten over all this—whatever it is. Can't you believe that it's you I love, whether or not you had polio? Can't you understand that the worst possible outcome for both of us is for you to take yourself away from me? I cannot bear to lose you—is there no getting that through to you? Bucky, your life can be so much easier if only you'll let it be. How do I convince you that we have to go on together? Don't save me, for God's sake. Do what we planned—marry me!"

But he wouldn't be budged, however much she cried and however heartfelt the crying seemed, even to him. "Marry me," she said, and he could only reply, "I will not do that to you," and she could only reply, "You're not doing anything to me— I am responsible for my decisions!" But there was no breaking down his opposition, not when his last opportunity to be a man of integrity was by sparing the virtuous young woman he dearly loved from unthinkingly taking a cripple as her mate for life. The only way to save a remnant of his honor was in denying himself everything he had ever wanted for himself—should he be weak enough to do otherwise, he would suffer his final defeat. Most important, if she was not already secretly relieved that he was rejecting her, if she was still too much under the sway of that loving innocence of hers—and under the sway as well of a morally punctilious father—to see the truth plainly for herself, she would feel differently when she had a family and a home of her own, with happy children and a husband who was whole. Yes, a day would come, and not far in the future, when she would find herself grateful to him for his having so pitilessly turned her away— when she would recognize how much better a life he had given her by his having vanished from it.

WHEN HE'D COMPLETED the story of the final meeting with Marcia, I asked him, "How bitter does all this leave you?"

"God killed my mother in childbirth. God gave me a thief for a father. In my early twenties, God gave me polio that I in turn gave to at least a dozen kids, probably more—including Marcia's sister, including you, most likely. Including Donald Kaplow. He died in an iron lung at Stroudsburg Hospital in August 1944. How bitter should I be? You tell me." He asserted this caustically, in the same tone in which he'd proclaimed that her God would one day betray Marcia and plant a knife in her back too.

"It's not for me," I replied, "to find fault with any polio sufferer, young or old, who can't fully overcome the pain of an infirmity that never ends. Of course there's brooding over its permanence. But there must in time be something more. You speak of God. You still believe in this God you disparage?"

"Yes. Somebody had to make this place."

"God the great criminal," I said. "Yet if it's God who's the criminal, it can't be you who's the criminal as well."

"Okay, it's a medical enigma. *I'm* a medical enigma," Bucky said confusingly. Did he mean perhaps that it was a *theological* enigma? Was this his Everyman's version of Gnostic doctrine, complete with an evil Demiurge? The divine as inimical to our being here? Admittedly, the evidence he could cull from his experience was not negligible. Only a fiend could invent polio. Only a fiend could invent Horace. Only a fiend could invent World War II. Add it all up and the fiend wins. The fiend is omnipotent. Bucky's conception of God, as I thought I understood it, was of an omnipotent being whose nature and purpose was to be adduced not from doubtful biblical evidence but from irrefutable historical proof, gleaned during a lifetime passed on this planet in the middle of the twentieth century. His conception of God was of an omnipotent being who was a union not of three persons in one Godhead, as in Christianity, but of two—a sick fuck and an evil genius.

To my atheistic mind, proposing such a God was certainly no more ridiculous than giving credence to the deities sustaining billions of others; as for Bucky's rebellion against Him, it struck me as absurd simply because there was no need for it. That the polio epidemic among the children of the Weequahic section and the children of Camp Indian Hill was a tragedy, he could not accept. He has to convert tragedy into guilt. He has to find a necessity for what happens. There is an epidemic and he needs a reason for it. He has to ask why. Why? Why? That it is pointless, contingent, preposterous, and tragic will not satisfy him. That it is a proliferating virus will not satisfy him. Instead he looks desperately for a deeper cause, this martyr, this maniac of the why, and finds the why either in God or in himself or, mystically, mysteriously, in their dreadful joining together as the sole destroyer. I have to say that however much I might sympathize with the amassing of woes that had blighted his life, this is nothing more than stupid hubris, not the hubris of will or desire but the hubris of fantastical, childish religious interpretation. We have heard it all before and by now have heard enough of it, even from someone as profoundly decent as Bucky Cantor.

"And you, Arnie?" he asked me. "You're without bitterness?"

"I got the disease when I was still a kid. I was twelve, about half your age. I was in the hospital for close to a year. I was the oldest one on the ward," I said, "surrounded by little kids screaming and crying for their families—day and night these little kids searching in vain for a face they knew. They weren't alone in feeling deserted. There was plenty of fear and despair to go around. And plenty of bitterness growing up with a pair of stick legs. For years I lay in bed at night talking to my limbs, whispering, 'Move! Move!' I missed a year of grade school, so when I got back, I had lost my class and my classmates. And in high school I had some hard knocks. The girls pitied me and the boys avoided me. I was always sitting brooding on the sidelines. Life on the sidelines makes for a painful adolescence. I wanted to walk like everyone else. Watching them, the unbroken ones, out after school playing ball, I wanted to shout, 'I have a right to be running too!' I was constantly torn by the thought that it could so eas-

ily have been another way. For a while I didn't want
to go to school at all—I didn't want to be reminded
all day long of what people my age looked like and
of all they could do. What I wanted was the tini-
est thing in the world: to be like everyone else. You
know the situation," I said to him. "I'll never be me
as I was me in the past. I'll be this instead for the
rest of my life. I'll never know delight again."

Bucky nodded. He who once, briefly, atop the
high board at Indian Hill, was the happiest man on
earth—who had listened to Marcia Steinberg ten-
derly lullabying him to sleep over the long-distance
line in the tremendous heat of that poisonous summer—understood all too easily what I was talking
about.

I told him then about a college roommate whom
I moved out on in my sophomore year. "When I
got to Rutgers," I said, "I was given the other Jewish polio victim to room with in the freshman dorm.
That's how Noah paired students up in those days.
This guy was physically far worse off than I was.
Grotesquely deformed. Boy named Pomerantz. A
brilliant scholarship student, high school valedicto-
rian, pre-med genius, and I couldn't stand him. He
drove me crazy. Couldn't shut up. Could never sti-

fle his all-consuming hunger for pre-polio Pomerantz. Could not elude for a single day the injustice
that had befallen him. Went ghoulishly on and on
about it. 'First you learn just what a cripple's life is
like,' he'd say to me. 'That's the first stage. When
you recover from that, you do what little is to be
done to avoid spiritual extinction. That's the second
stage. After that, you struggle not to be nothing but
your ordeal all the while that's all you're becom-
ing. Then, if you're lucky, five hundred stages later,
sometime in your seventies, you find you are finally
able to say with some truth, "Well, I managed after
all—I did not allow the life to be sucked out of me
completely." That's when you die.' Pomerantz did
great in college, easily got into medical school, and
then *he* died—in his first year there he killed himself."

"I can't say," Bucky told me, "that I wasn't once
attracted by the idea myself."

"I thought about it too," I said. "But then I wasn't
quite the mess that Pomerantz was. And then I got
lucky, tremendously lucky: in the last year of college I met my wife. And slowly polio ceased to be
the only drama, and I got weaned away from rail-
ing at my fate. I learned that back there in Weequa-

hic in 1944 I'd lived through a summerlong social tragedy that didn't have to be a lifelong personal tragedy too. My wife's been a tender, laughing companion for eighteen years. She's counted for a lot. And having children to father, you begin to forget the hand you've been dealt."

"I'm sure that's true. You look like a contented man."

"Where are you living now?" I asked.

"I moved to North Newark. I moved near Branch Brook Park. The furniture at my grandmother's place was so old and creaky that I didn't bother to keep it. Went out one Saturday morning and bought a brand-new bed, sofa, chairs, lamps, everything. I've got a comfortable place."

"What do you do for socializing?"

"I'm not much of a socializer, Arnie. I go to the movies. I go down to the Ironbound on Sundays for a good Portuguese meal. I enjoy sitting in the park when it's nice. I watch TV. I watch the news."

I thought of him doing these things by himself and, like a lovesick swain, attempting on Sundays not to pine for Marcia Steinberg or to imagine during the week that he'd seen her, age twenty-two, walking on one of the downtown streets. One would have predicted, remembering the young man he'd been, that he would have had the strength to battle through to something more than this. And then I thought of myself without my family, and wondered if I would have done any better or even as well. Movies and work and Sunday dinner out—it sounded awfully bleak to me.

"Do you watch sports?"

Vigorously he shook his head as though I'd asked a child if he played with matches.

"I understand," I said. "When my kids were very young and I couldn't run around the yard with them, and when they were older and learned to ride bikes and I couldn't ride with them, it got to me. You try to choke down your feelings but it isn't easy."

"I don't even read the sports pages in the paper. I don't want to see them."

"Did you ever see your friend Dave when he came back from the war?"

"He got a job in the Englewood school system. He took his wife and his kids and he moved up there. No, I don't see him." Then he lapsed into silence, and it couldn't have been clearer that despite his stoical claim that what he did not have he lived without, he had not in the least accustomed himself to having lost so much, and that twenty-seven years later, he wondered still about all that had and had not happened, trying his best not to think of a multitude of things—among them, that by now he would have been head of the athletic program at Weequahic High.

"I wanted to help kids and make them strong," he finally said, "and instead I did them irrevocable harm." That was the thought that had shaped his decades of silent suffering, a man who was himself the least deserving of harm. He looked at that moment as if he had lived on this earth seven thousand shameful years. I took hold of his good hand then—a hand whose muscles worked well enough but that was no longer substantial and strong, a hand with no more firmness to it than a piece of soft fruit—and I said, "*Polio* did them the harm. You weren't a perpetrator. You had as little to do with spreading it as Horace did. You were just as much a victim as any of us was."

"Not so, Arnie. I remember one night Bill Blomback telling the kids about the Indians, telling them how the Indians believed that it was an evil being, shooting them with an invisible arrow, that caused certain of their diseases—"

"Don't," I protested. "Don't go any further with that, please. It's a campfire story, Bucky, a story for kids. There's probably a medicine man in it who drives off evil spirits. You're *not* the Indians' evil being. You were not the arrow, either, damn it—you were not the bringer of crippling and death. If you ever were a perpetrator—if you won't give ground about that—I repeat: you were a totally blameless one."

Then, vehemently—as though I could bring about change in him merely by a tremendous desire to do so; as though, after all our hours of talking over lunch, I could now get him to see himself as something more than his deficiencies and begin to liquidate his shame; as though it were within my power to revive a remnant of the unassailable young playground director who, unaided by anyone, had warded off the ten Italian roughnecks intending to frighten us with the threat of spreading polio among the Jews—I said, "Don't be against yourself. There's enough cruelty in the world as it is. Don't make things worse by scapegoating yourself."

But there's nobody less salvageable than a ruined good boy. He'd been alone far too long with his sense of things—and without all he'd wanted so desperately to have—for me to dislodge his interpretation of his life's terrible event or to shift his relation with it. Bucky wasn't a brilliant man—he wouldn't have had to be one to teach phys ed to kids—nor was he ever in the least carefree. He was largely a humorless person, articulate enough but with barely a trace of wit, who never in his life had spoken satirically or with irony, who rarely cracked a joke or spoke in jest—someone instead haunted by an exacerbated sense of duty but endowed with little force of mind, and for that he had paid a high price in assigning the gravest meaning to his story, one that, intensifying over time, perniciously magnified his misfortune. The havoc that had been wrought both on the Chancellor playground and at Indian Hill seemed to him not a malicious absurdity of nature but a great crime of his own, costing him all he'd once possessed and wrecking his life. The guilt in someone like Bucky may seem absurd but, in fact, is unavoidable. Such a person is condemned. Nothing he does matches the ideal in him. He never knows where his responsibility ends. He never trusts his limits because, saddled with a stern natural goodness that will not permit him to resign himself to the suffering of others, he will never guiltlessly acknowledge that he has any limits. Such a person's greatest triumph is in sparing his beloved from having a crippled husband, and his heroism consists of denying his deepest desire by relinquishing her.

Though maybe if he hadn't fled the challenge of the playground, maybe if he hadn't abandoned the Chancellor kids only days before the city shut down the playground and sent them all home—and maybe, too, if his closest buddy hadn't been killed in the war—he would not have been so quick to blame himself for the cataclysm and might not have become one of those people taken to pieces by his times. Maybe if he had stayed on and outlasted polio's communal testing of the Weequahic Jews, and, regardless of whatever might have happened to him, had manfully seen the epidemic through to the end . . .

Or maybe he would have come to see it his way no matter where he'd been, and for all I know—for all the science of epidemiology knows—maybe rightly so. Maybe Bucky wasn't mistaken. Maybe he wasn't deluded by self-mistrust. Maybe his assertions weren't exaggerated and he hadn't drawn the wrong conclusion. Maybe he *was* the invisible arrow.

AND YET, at twenty-three, he was, to all of us boys, the most exemplary and revered authority we knew, a young man of convictions, easygoing, kind, fair-minded, thoughtful, stable, gentle, vigorous, muscular—a comrade and leader both. And never a more glorious figure than on the afternoon near the end of June, before the '44 epidemic seriously took hold in the city—before, for more than a few of us, our bodies and our lives would be drastically transformed—when we all marched behind him to the big dirt field across the street and down a short slope from the playground. It was where the high school football team held its workouts and practices and where he was going to show us how to throw the javelin. He was dressed in his skimpy, satiny track shorts and his sleeveless top, he wore cleated shoes, and, leading the pack, he carried the javelin loosely in his right hand.

When we got down to the field it was empty, and Mr. Cantor had us gather together on the sidelines

at the Chancellor Avenue end, where he let us each
examine the javelin and heft it in our hands, a slender metal pole weighing a little under two pounds
and measuring about eight and a half feet long. He
showed us the various holds you could use on the
whipcord grip and then the one that he preferred.
Then he explained to us something about the background of the javelin, which began in early socie-
ties, before the invention of the bow and arrow, with
the throwing of the spear for hunting, and continued in Greece at the first Olympics in the eighth
century B.C. The first javelin thrower was said to
be Hercules, the great warrior and slayer of mon-
sters, who, Mr. Cantor told us, was the giant son
of the supreme Greek god, Zeus, and the strongest
man on earth. The lecture over, he said he would
now do his warm-ups, and we watched while he
limbered up for about twenty minutes, some of the
boys on the sidelines doing their best to mimic his
movements. It was important, he said—at the same
time as he was performing a side split with his pel-
vis to the ground—always to work beforehand at
stretching the groin muscles, which were easily sus-
ceptible to strain. He used the javelin as a stretching
stick for many of the exercises, twisting and turn-

ing with it balanced like a yoke across his shoulders
while he kneeled and squatted and lunged and then
while he stood and flexed and rotated his torso. He
did a handstand and began walking a wide circle on
his hands, and some of the kids tried that; with his
mouth only inches from the ground, he informed
us that he was doing the handstands in lieu of ex-
ercising on a bar to stretch his upper body. He finished off with forward body bends and trunk back-
bends, during which he kept his heels fixed to the
ground while pushing upward with his hips and
arching his back amazingly high. When he said he
was going to sprint twice around the edge of the
field, we followed, barely able to keep up with him
but pretending that it was we who were warming
up for the throw. Then for a few minutes he practiced running along an imaginary runway without
throwing the javelin, just carrying it high, flat, and
straight.

When he was ready to begin, he told us what to
watch for, starting with his approach run and the
bounding stride and ending with the throw. Without the javelin in his hand he walked through the
entire delivery for us in slow motion, describing it
as he did so. "It's not magic, boys, and it's no picnic

either. However, if you practice hard," he said, "and you work hard and you exercise diligently—if you're regular with your balance drills, one, your mobility drills, two, and your flexibility drills, three—if you're faithful to your weight-training program, and if throwing the javelin really matters to you, I guarantee you, something will come of it. Everything in sports requires determination. The three D's. Determination, dedication, and discipline, and you're practically all the way there."

As usual, taking every precaution, he told us that for safety's sake no one was to dart out onto the field at any point; we were to watch everything from where we were standing. He made this point twice. He couldn't have been more serious, the seriousness being the expression of his commitment to the task.

And then he hurled the javelin. You could see each of his muscles bulging when he released it into the air. He let out a strangulated yowl of effort (one we all went around imitating for days afterward), a noise expressing the essence of him—the naked battle cry of striving excellence. The instant the javelin took flight from his hand, he began dancing about to recover his balance and not fall across the foul line he'd etched in the dirt with his cleats. And all the while he watched the javelin as it made its trajectory in a high, sweeping arc over the field. None of us had ever before seen an athletic act so beautifully executed right in front of our eyes. The javelin carried, carried way beyond the fifty-yard line, down to the far side of the opponent's thirty, and when it descended and landed, the shaft quivered and its pointed metal tip angled sharply into the ground from the sailing force of the flight.

We sent up a loud cheer and began leaping about. All of the javelin's trajectory had originated in Mr. Cantor's supple muscles. His was the body—the feet, the legs, the buttocks, the trunk, the arms, the shoulders, even the thick stump of the bull neck— that acting in unison had powered the throw. It was as though our playground director had turned into a primordial man, hunting for food on the plains where he foraged, taming the wilds by the might of his hand. Never were we more in awe of anyone. Through him, we boys had left the little story of the neighborhood and entered the historical saga of our ancient gender.

He threw the javelin repeatedly that afternoon, each throw smooth and powerful, each throw accompanied by that resounding mingling of a shout and a grunt, and each, to our delight, landing several yards farther down the field than the last. Running with the javelin aloft, stretching his throwing arm back behind his body, bringing the throwing arm through to release the javelin high over his shoulder—and releasing it then like an explosion—he seemed to us invincible.

In 1997 Philip Roth won the Pulitzer Prize for *American Pastoral*. In 1998 he received the National Medal of Arts at the White House and in 2002 the highest award of the American Academy of Arts and Letters, the Gold Medal in Fiction, previously awarded to John Dos Passos, William Faulkner, and Saul Bellow, among others. He has twice won the National Book Award and the National Book Critics Circle Award. He has won the PEN/Faulkner Award three times. In 2005 *The Plot Against America* received the Society of American Historians' prize for "the outstanding historical novel on an American theme for 2003–2004." He has also won American PEN's two highest awards: the PEN/Nabokov and the PEN/Bellow. He is the only living American novelist to have his work published in a comprehensive, definitive edition by the Library of America. The last of nine volumes is scheduled for publication in 2013.